Chapters

By Mark Milne

Cover: Klöntalersee, Kanton Glarus,
Switzerland

www.markpmilne.com

For Xenia

Chapters

Manuel y Rosa

Manuel looked again at his ticket for the number of the cabin that was reserved in his name. It was only the third time he had had to look at it. Why could he not remember even one simple number? A number and a letter. Seat 106G. Was that so difficult? He was unsatisfied with himself.

Vera.

What would Vera have said? What would she have done? If you told Vera the number – number and letter – only one time, you would not have to tell her again for one hundred years. You could ask her on her 100th birthday: What was your seat number on the train to Lima on July 30, 1936? She would look you in the eye and say, 'Well, it was 106G, of course.'

Always 'of course'. Kicking a man when he was down. Manuel came to his own defense now. He had been up since five in the morning. He was fine for some hours but now was beginning to feel the weight of the late night out entertaining a client, combined with a poor night of sleep, combined with having woken up so early. *¡Caray!* Who would have had a sharp memory under these conditions? He felt vindicated for an instant, before the answer arrived. Vera could.

To hell with Vera. It was long over. He had to stop thinking about her. He needed something to take her place.

'Excuse me,' he said, as the door to a cabin opened suddenly and he nearly collided with its occupant who had propelled himself into the aisle without looking. Manuel set

1

his bag down behind him as the man squeezed by, allowing his shoulder muscles to relax briefly under the sudden absence of the burden. It was hot in the train. It was hot outside. Manuel felt the sweat on his brow under the wool hat. *Why a wool hat in summer,* he could hear Vera asking. *Yes, damn you, I grabbed the wrong hat in my haste as I left home. A thousand pardons.*

Enough.

A moment later Manuel was off again, having glanced at the number of the cabin the man had emerged from. *Okay, 96A-F, keep going.* The smell of old oil took hold of him as he pressed on. Old oil, steel, coal and grease. The smells of a train in the station. It would dissolve once the locomotive departed. The fresh air from a partially opened window would bring other, more pleasant smells to him. The pine trees, the ocean. *Don't worry. Just find your cabin and get situated.* Then there would be nothing to do but rest, sleep, read. Perhaps chat with a cabin mate. Perhaps not. That would depend on many things.

That was the only thing to look forward to on these business trips. A piece of freedom. Some spare time with no phone, no typewriter, no paperwork. This trip would be no different. *Relax.*

He passed through the car and entered the next one. This must be the last one, he thought. And it was. And his cabin, the last one, in the last car, a car with surprisingly few passengers in it, finally appeared. He looked through the glass doors apprehensively as he approached the cabin. To his relief, it was empty. He opened one of the doors, threw his hat into the cabin where it landed safely on the bench, and then opened the other door. *Maybe I'll get lucky and no one else will come.* He stepped inside and lifted his suitcase up onto the storage shelf above the seat.

The train whistle let go just then with one long blast. Five minutes to departure. The next time it would be two shorter blasts, signaling the one minute mark, and then it would be under way. Manuel removed his coat and hung it on the elaborate brass hook in one of the cabin's corners, and sat on the bench with his back towards the front of the train. He thought to slide over towards the window, then remained in the middle of the bench where he was. There would be time to move over later. As he heard the two final blasts of the train's whistle he closed his eyes, overcome by fatigue.

In his dream he stood at the base of a perfectly green hill, as round as could be, topped by lush shade trees. To his left sat a wooden bench. A breeze carried the scent of unseen flowers to him. He gazed at the hilltop. He was drawn to it, and wanted to amble up the slope to the trees above. He did not know why, but felt its pull all the same. He was about to begin the walk over the emerald colored grassy slope when he was struck by an odd sensation, one that told him that he could not do it. That it was out of reach for him to attempt. He turned then suddenly, and eyed the bench as if it had called his name. It seemed an easy alternative, and the idea of sitting and admiring the hill and surroundings appealed to him. He sat on the old wooden bench and gripped the armrest with his hand. Rough and dry, it contrasted with the softness all around him. He looked at the wood under his arm and then the wood grain turned into scales and the arms and legs of the bench into snakes that began to twitch and writhe underneath him.

He opened his eyes. All was quiet. Still. The train. It was no longer moving. He sat forward and looked out of the window. They had arrived at the first stop. Passengers were coming and going. He took his timepiece out of his pocket, holding it by its chain, then gripping the body of the watch and pressing the button that opened the silver case. It was just after noon. Manuel closed the watch and rubbed some life into his face. He stood up and stepped over to the window, looking outside. It was a small town. Hardly worth the time to stop, he thought. He yawned and bent forward to touch his toes. Something his doctor had told him about recently in order to stave off headaches and depression. Eat well, sleep well, and stretch every day. Loosening up the muscles kept the body from developing logjams which in turn produced headaches and an unhealthy outlook on life.

With his fingertips on the toes of his brown leather shoes, he closed his eyes. Suddenly the door behind him opened and he saw, between his legs, two feet on the floor behind him. They were the feet of a woman. 'Pardon me,' the woman said.

Manuel quickly stood bolt upright and smoothed his hair with both hands. 'Oh, of course,' he said. He stepped aside and allowed the woman to enter. She was short, wore a dark skirt and coat and hat, and held herself very stiff and erect. Like someone used to being examined. She had a violent beauty about her, he noticed. A fierceness in her face, in the shape of it, with heavy, dark eyebrows, full and sharply contoured lips, and a rather large, powerful nose. Not wide, but a bit long. A prow on the ship of an icebreaker. But her eyes betrayed the rest of her. For they were soft, deep brown, large, and yes, gentle. Such a gentleness in her eyes like he had never seen. All her other features gathered round the softness of her eyes, her self, her true soul, to guard and protect her. Manuel saw a thin line of perspiration on her forehead. The woman held her ticket in one hand. A small bag in the other. She looked at her ticket and said the number of the cabin aloud. The both of them stood, examining their surroundings. 'Please,' Manuel said at once, 'Sit anywhere you like. We are alone here.' He gestured to the two benches which sat facing each other. The woman's soft eyes looked directly into his. He held his breath. 'Shall I take your bag?' he asked her.

'No,' she told him. 'Thank you.'

As Manuel stood with his back to his own bench, the woman simply sat opposite him and placed her bag next to her. Manuel sat down then as well. The woman removed her hat and placed it on her bag, then pulled a white kerchief from her coat and patted her brow, then her cheeks, and finally her upper lip and her chin. Manuel did not miss any of this. When she was finished, she put her kerchief back into her coat and looked once again at Manuel. Manuel nodded. 'I am Manuel Garcia de la Vasquez,' he told her, rising then slightly and extending his hand to her. She did not take her eyes off him. She leaned forward and took his hand in hers and nodded. Manuel felt something stir within him as he felt her warm hand in his. He released her hand, feeling that perhaps he had been revealed to her, and unwilling to be exposed in such a way so suddenly upon their meeting.

'I am Rosa,' the woman said simply, as she watched Manuel withdraw his hand.

With this formality accomplished, Rosa sat back and unbuttoned her coat, then fixed her gaze on a point outside the window, raising her arm as she did and resting it on the sill. Manuel looked outside as well, as if invited to share in her examination of the world outside. But it was soon apparent that he had not been so invited, and at that point he folded his hands together in his lap and looked at them, bowing his head slightly.

Rosa watched as the platform conductor raised his hand, looked down the platform, and nodded. A man at work. Two short blasts from the train's whistle sounded. The man walked away, removing the cap from his head. Rosa turned her head and looked at the man seated in front of her. He seemed to be a kind man. She felt sure of it. But she knew that it could turn out to be otherwise. She sensed that he was patient as well. Educated, from his general appearance and from his manner. Her thoughts drifted to Juan, her lover, and to her husband who had killed him exactly one year ago. She no longer missed Juan. She knew this, and it troubled her. *Where is my eternal love?* The man before her was younger than Juan. Younger than her husband even, who now would sit in prison for the remainder of his life. He was not yet thirty years old.

'Are you also headed for Lima?' she asked Manuel.

Manuel looked up at her and placed his hands on his knees. 'Yes, all the way down,' he smiled. Rosa saw that he had a nice smile. Not the smile of a waiter in a restaurant, trying to draw someone in. Not like her husband. She had been so young then. Too young, apparently, to have been able to be wise in such matters. And he had been considerably older, and somewhat clever. Someone had given him a version of what a woman wanted to hear and he had used that advice to entice her. It had worked, so she could not say anything against it now. Only that she had been young and not clever enough. Her older and wiser eyes looked Manuel over. *Who cares if he can see me? I am an experienced woman. He must learn.* But when his smile faltered, when his open and trusting expression turned to one of caution, to one that was in the process of learning one of life's lessons without being thankful for it, Rosa abruptly felt shame and forced her eyes to look once more outside at the train platform. The train began moving again.

Manuel had not liked the way the woman looked at him. He had not been sure just how it was that she had looked at him. Had not known what it was that she was trying to accomplish. But he had been unnerved by her intrusive gaze, and had felt shame at his reaction, with her being a woman, and he a man. Should he not have been in control of just that sort of situation? What was the matter with him? He studied her face freely now as she looked out the window. She took no notice of him. He wished then that she would notice his stare so that he could keep it fixed on her to show that he could also be intimidating. Perhaps, being a pretty woman, she had developed an indifference to receiving such attention. Suddenly he felt foolish. Perhaps there had been no significance whatsoever in how she had watched him. Perhaps he was seeing something that was not there. The woman stood and removed her coat as Manuel watched her. She paid him no attention until she had finished hanging up her coat on the rack next to the door behind the bench and sat down again. Then she looked at him and smiled.

'It's not so hot today as it has been,' she said. 'But it's still a bit warm here in the cabin.'

Manuel nodded. Both of them looked at the window then, and then at the sign above it. *Do not open*, it read. They looked at each other. The woman smiled once more. 'There can't be any harm in opening the window,' Manuel said, and he stood up and released the latch above the frame and lowered the window until a refreshing breeze filled the cabin. The two of them smiled conspiratorially.

'Thank you,' the woman said.

The day passed. Soon after the train had again departed, lunch had been brought to the first-class passengers in the cabins. Manuel and Rosa had exchanged only few words over their meal. Manuel had learned that Rosa was one year older than he – not because he had asked her, of course, but in fact because she had asked him and then had commented on the difference in their ages. He also learned that following some kind of unpleasantness or other which she was not interested in explaining, she was on her way to live with her parents in Lima and to resettle there. Rosa had shown no interest in Manuel's profession when he had explained to her that he sold building equipment for a national construction firm. And what special interest should she have shown? Well, none, of course. After lunch Manuel had again fallen asleep. So had Rosa.

In the late afternoon a delay at a scheduled stop occurred. They would be waylaid for at least an hour, they had been informed, due to a fault in the track switching mechanism. Rosa left the train to have a look around while Manuel remained on board and read from a book of European history that he had brought with him. 'It's a shame that we cannot go together,' Rosa had said before leaving. Someone needed to remain on the train to watch over their belongings. Manuel had been surprised, and pleased, at her comment. He could tell that she had meant it. He read his book in peace on the train, but found his mind wandering to the woman with the soft eyes and full lips.

Before he knew it the train whistle began to sound and the conductor on the platform called out to the crowd. The train would be leaving shortly. Sitting alone in the cabin, Manuel became anxious as the minutes ticked by and Rosa did not appear. He lowered the window completely now and stood searching the platform for her. He leaned out of the window and looked up and then down the platform but did not see her. He turned and looked at her bag on the bench and frowned. What was the matter? The train had been delayed for more than one hour now. Rosa should have returned. He went to the window again and looked up and down the platform once more. He had filled his lungs with air and was about to call out her name in desperation when he heard something behind him. He pulled his head inside the train and spun around. Rosa stood at the door with a look on her face that matched his own surprise. Manuel was instantly embarrassed to have been caught in such a state of agitation, but that sentiment was erased when Rosa smiled at him.

'Sorry,' she said. 'It seems I nearly missed the train.'

'Yes,' Manuel agreed. 'Nearly.' Rosa explained that she had lost her way after having spent some time waiting to have her coat pocket repaired. As the train began to pull out of the station, Rosa's relief at having managed to find her way back on time turned to despair as she discovered that she had lost her money purse.

'I must have left it in the shop,' she cried. Luckily she had not brought her identification card, train tickets and other valuables with her. 'It's only money,' she said, 'but it is all that I had.'

Manuel tried to reassure her. 'There are no more stops now until we reach Lima,' he said. 'But if you need something, just tell me.'

Manuel had imagined that Rosa might be more talkative now on the last leg of their journey but instead she was oddly quiet. Even distant. He occupied himself with his book but merely went round and round. As the sky outside darkened, he tried to forget about it. As the train rocked from side to side he stole glances at her: as she read her own book, as she rummaged through her bag now and then, as she napped. He found himself wanting her. He imagined what it would be like to look into her brown eyes as their lips met and he pressed himself against her. He nodded off and his imagination of Rosa found him in his sleep. He dreamt of her. He dreamt of falling into her warmth and feeling something glowing inside him that seemed to promise a new beginning for him. A new life. The one he had always dreamed of.

At once Rosa awoke to see Manuel asleep on the bench opposite her. She stretched and watched as the first stars of the night shone on them outside their window. Looking back at Manuel, she saw that his sleep did not appear to be entirely peaceful. A faint expression of displeasure crossed his face, then faltered. On an impulse she rose and sat next to him. With him this close to her, his beauty had an altogether different effect on her and before she knew it she found herself reaching out to touch him. With one finger she traced the line of his upper lip. His face softened under her touch. She sat watching him for a time before rising quietly to take her seat, where she continued to observe him in his peaceful slumber.

'Manuel. Manuel,' she called to him, her hand on his arm, urging him to awaken.

He opened his eyes and for one brilliant instant saw only her face and thought his dreams had all come true.

'The train,' she said, her expression worried. 'Something has broken. They say we will not be able to continue until tomorrow. We've stopped and must find lodging. What will I do? I have nothing.'

Manuel took a deep breath and sat up straight, then stood up and looked out the window at the platform teaming with people as the passengers made their way off the stricken locomotive.

'We must leave,' Rosa told him.

Manuel looked at her and took his suitcase down from the rack overhead. 'Don't worry, Rosa, you will come with me,' he told her. 'Come, I must speak with one of the conductors, and if it is as you say, then I will find us an accommodation and everything will be all right.'

'But I have no money,' Rosa pleaded.

'Nonsense. Don't you trouble yourself,' Manuel told her. 'I will take care of it. But we have to get moving now before the other passengers snap up all the available rooms.'

Manuel and Rosa hurried off of the train and into the night in search of a place to stay. At Manuel's insistence they passed by the Hotel Mayor directly across from the station and went further on towards a large hotel that was brightly lit and flew many colorful flags outside its entrance. This hotel was much less busy than the first one, but clearly more expensive too. Manuel went directly to the front desk, with Rosa at his side. Before he could speak, however, he was informed that the hotel was fully booked.

'I am sorry sir,' the man behind the counter told him, 'but we have no more rooms available. A train, you see –'

'Yes,' Manuel interrupted. 'I know. We have come from the train ourselves.'

'Ah,' the man said, shaking his head apologetically.

'Have you nothing at all?' Manuel pleaded.

'Well, we do have the honeymoon suite, but –'

At those words, Manuel thought of Vera, and realized that he hadn't thought of her once since meeting Rosa.

He smiled. 'We'll take it,' Manuel told him, and he turned and caught Rosa's eye and nodded once to her. And it was done. Manuel signed the register and a porter appeared at his side. Taking their bags, he led them up the stairs to their room. He unlocked the door and proceeded into the room, placing the bags on a stand near a large closet and then showing them the lounge, bathroom, bedroom and finally the balcony. The porter remained on the balcony and beckoned to Manuel and Rosa to join him. He pointed to the west. 'From here,' he told them, 'you can see clear to the ocean.' Manuel gave the young man a tip and thanked him. As the porter left the room and closed the door quietly behind him, Rosa advanced to the railing of the balcony. A breeze blew through her hair as she gripped the wrought iron and stared into the blackness in the direction of the sea.

'I want to see the ocean,' she said.

Manuel approached her, then stopped two paces behind her. She pushed her coat off of her shoulders and let it slide down her arms into Manuel's waiting hands. Then, without turning, she slowly handed him her hat. Then her blouse. She stepped out of her shoes. She unfastened her skirt and let it fall, then stepped out of it and handed it back where it was received and removed. Finally she stood naked at the railing. Her hands went up to untie the ribbon that held up her hair.

'No,' Manuel told her, 'let me.'

Rosa stood erect and clasped her hands together behind her back, expectantly. Noticing this, Manuel hesitated, then continued with the red ribbon until it was off and Rosa's dark, silky hair spilled down her back. Manuel took the ribbon and looped it once, then twice around Rosa's wrists before tying the ends fast. He placed his hands on Rosa's shoulders, then moved his fingertips down gently to her elbows where he paused, then reached forward and held her breasts in his hands, feeling her nipples stiffen under his touch. He stepped forward and pulled her close to him. Rosa was surprised to feel his nakedness on her back as he drew her to him and caressed her cheek with his lips as he inhaled deeply. His shudder ran through the both of them so that Rosa could not be sure that it was not her own.

Manuel stepped back from Rosa and turned her around on the balcony to face him. 'You are a goddess,' he told her.

She smiled. 'And I am not a dream,' she said.

Rosa awoke in the night and turned over in the bed to find Manuel fast asleep. She watched him breathing slowly. Peacefully. *My life is too complicated. Too much trouble for such a decent man. In the morning, I will tell him. I will make something up. Tell him that I have someone waiting for me.* She was careful not to wake him with her tears. Then suddenly he turned and reached out for her in his sleep, taking hold of her around the waist and pulling her close to him.

In the morning Manuel was awakened by the breeze that came in through the open balcony doors. Lying in the bed, he looked out across the spacious room that he did not immediately recognize. He thought of Rosa and sat up quickly. He saw his suitcase on the stand by the closet, but not hers. He threw the sheet off of him and stood up, looking back at the bed behind him, open mouthed, half panicked.

Rosa! Where did she go? How could she have just left me? He looked at the door and then back at the bed, as if looking again, starting over, could deliver a new reality. Staring at the bed, Manuel noticed something dark in the sheets. He rubbed his eyes and took one step forward. It was a lock of dark hair protruding from under the sheet he had so roughly tossed aside. It was all he could do to keep from falling apart, one limb after another, as he felt an immense rush of relief, joy and love overwhelm him. Trembling, he knelt down on the soft mattress and took the sheet in his hand and gently pulled it back to find Rosa lying there. He slipped into bed next to her, placing his hand on her hip, and drinking in the smell of the woman he vowed then and there to marry. He fell asleep caressing a lock of her silky hair with his fingertips. And he dreamed.

Ton of Bricks

Tim Skinner peered cautiously out of his living room window.

Nobody around.

Not that he had anything to hide, or that it was unusual for him to be looking out his own window. Out of this particular window. In fact, this was the window he used to keep an eye on his kids when they were there, at the Millers'.

Their backyards were parallel to one another, and since the Millers' house was on land that was a kind of step down from his own, lower by three or four feet, and since there was no fence separating the two properties, he could easily see over into their yard. It was great, actually. With the kids never content to play in one of the two yards for very long, he could never be sure where they were. It was good to be able to look outside and spot them. You had to be careful. If you didn't keep your eye on them, before you knew it they'd wiggle their way out through that one damned hole – in the Millers' hedge, of course, not his own – and out into the street. And even though they lived on a quiet little ring road off the beaten track and there was little traffic other than neighbor traffic, some of them, and not only those who didn't have kids, drove too darned fast. So he was glad to have this window to keep tabs on things.

He didn't have to feel guilty looking out that window into the neighbors' yard but in this case, because of his reason for looking, he wasn't merely looking, the way he normally did. He was peering. Peering to see it, and to contemplate the situation it had created.

There it was. That towering concoction, standing proudly on the lawn in the corner of the yard all alone. Must have been nearly eight feet tall. Ridiculous. A *barbecue*, for God's sake. Just a barbecue. An eight foot tall cement barbecue that he was now certain posed a threat. Not only to the Millers, but, since he spent a fair amount of time there in their back yard, to himself as well. But of course, it was the children that he was really concerned about. His precious children.

The question was, how to deal with it?

He remembered the first time he saw it, when Don and Nancy Miller had returned from their trip down south where they had bought the thing and had it shipped so that their return had coincided with its arrival. He hadn't seen them unload it. That must have been interesting. It came in several chunks, with the base and the central piece – what would you call it? – the *fireplace,* being easily the heaviest pieces. How many people had they needed for that job? He hadn't even seen Don putting it together, as a matter of fact. If he had, he might not have found himself in this situation. He might have been able to recommend a better way of constructing a base for the thing to sit on.

It certainly was plausible. After all, Don and Nancy respected his opinion on things like that after he fixed their back yard gate. He couldn't help it, having seen it sit there for months, unable to be opened, while they stepped over it, handed children back and forth over it, day in and day out. It wasn't even that hard a job. Just a little realignment of the hinges. He didn't know if Don had just been lazy, or if he really couldn't figure out how to fix it. Don was no fool. He had graduated from college with a degree in economics, after all. That must have meant something, even though he was a big ox of a man and laughed like he did, easily and loudly. Almost constantly, it seemed to Tim sometimes. So often that his wife Sandra would say to him, as they sat together in the living room or at the dinner table 'Oh, listen to Don! He's so funny!'

Tim remembered the first time he met Don, shortly after they had moved in. His wife had already met Nancy one day when several of the parents were out in the street keeping an eye on their younger children as they played. He had gone over with his son and daughter after Don had seen them looking down into their yard at his own children and asked him if he'd like to have a beer with him and let the kids play together. Shaking hands with him in his back yard, knocking their beers together and having a drink, Don had struck Tim again as friendly and unassuming. As the kind of guy you'd want to have as a neighbor.

He had just accepted the chair Don had motioned for him to sit in under the awning on the patio when Don's smile got the better of him and he erupted once more into a bouncing laugh.

'Your wife told Nancy that you called me a caveman,' he said, obviously finding the incident greatly amusing.

Tim's mouth nearly fell open. The hair on the back of his neck bristled. He knew Sandra and Nancy had met. Sandra had mentioned it, and had said what a nice woman Nancy had seemed to be. She failed, however, to tell him that she had informed the wife of the burly man who now sat smiling at him that he and Sandra had nicknamed Don 'The Caveman,' based on his general appearance and his penchant for barbecuing, and mainly because of the impression he gave them the first time they saw him standing at the grill – the one they had before they got the big one – in his back yard one afternoon dressed only in his leopard print bathing suit.

It could have been meant as a trap, but after the initial shock left him, Tim realized that Don hadn't meant it that way at all. He was clearly not bothered by what Sandra had said in the least. Tim managed to laugh it off, thinking to himself all the while 'I'm going to strangle Sandra. That's it. I'm just going to strangle her.'

There was no doubt that the Millers were the nicest people on the block. Tim and Sandra hadn't managed to connect as well with anyone else as they had with Don and Nancy. Despite their eccentricities, they were, after all, just nice people. Nice people with a huge barbecue in their back yard that was going to fall on top of someone someday and kill them.

As he stood there at the window staring at it, Tim made up his mind. He had to do something about it. He just needed a game plan.

'Tim?' he heard his wife calling to him from the basement. 'Tim! Can you help me for a minute?'

Taking a last look at the deadly barbecue, Tim stepped back from the window and turned toward the door of the living room.

'Coming!'

It took him completely off guard, when Don hollered up at him suddenly from his back yard.

'Tim! Hi!'

Tim sat in one of the lawn chairs reading a section of the Sunday paper. Sandra sat nearby with her own piece of it, in her bathing suit, soaking up the sun. Tim looked at Don over his paper. 'Hey Don, how's it going?'

'Great. Fine. Hey, listen, why don't you all come over for a barbecue for lunch?'

A barbecue? The barbecue! The *barbecue*! Jesus, how had he forgotten about it? It was a couple of weeks ago when he'd set his mind to it, and what had happened? Nothing, that's what. Nada.

He looked at Sandra, who made a 'why not?' face at him and then went back to her paper.

'Sure Don. Sounds great. Shall we bring anything?' Tim asked, folding his paper and tossing it on the lawn next to where he lay.

'Nah, I'm all set. Just bring yourselves, that's enough. About one? One-thirty?'

Tim waited once more for a sign from his wife. 'Sounds good.' He got up and swore quietly.

'What?' Sandra asked him.

'Oh, nothing,' Tim told her. Then he was suddenly seized by the urge to tell Sandra about the Millers' barbecue and sat down quickly on his chair, leaning forward and calling her to do the same with his eyes.

'What?' Sandra whispered.

'Don's barbecue. Have you seen the base of it? How sloppily he put it together?'

Sensing the loss of what she had hoped would be a tantalizing piece of gossip, Sandra's expectant grin disappeared before she glared at her husband. 'No, why? And who cares, anyway?'

'Who cares?' Don cried, looking once over his shoulder into the Millers' yard and being careful to lower his voice. 'I care! Listen, that thing is dangerous, I tell you. He didn't use enough cement between the bricks. They're hollow, you know, and if you line them up you get a nice big tube down the middle,' he said, his energy waning as Sandra's expression turned to one of incomprehension. What am I doing, he thought. She won't understand. She obviously doesn't care. Why can't she understand this kind of thing anyway? Building things, and normal physics. It's just common sense! 'The thing could topple over and kill someone!' he hissed.

'Oh, stop it, Tim. Gosh. Really.'

'I'm serious.'

But it was too late. With her head tucked behind her paper, Sandra had already forgotten about Don's out-of-control barbecue. Tim watched her read for a minute and then glanced at the gleaming white tower next door. Suddenly Sandra lowered her paper.

'Don't you say anything to Don, you hear me? That would just be *so* embarrassing, Tim, if you made a scene about Don's barbecue, for Christ's sake! Promise me now. Promise me? Tim!'

'Yeah, all right! Jesus! Leave me alone.'

'Don't say anything to him,' Sandra warned him once more through her newspaper. Moments later she set it down and leaned back, closing her eyes against the sun's rays. 'Are you going inside?' she asked.

Tim looked at her. What would she need now? 'No,' he said.

'Would you get me some sun block?'

Tim waited a moment and then pushed himself up and out of his chair before going into the house through the open sliding glass door. 'Sure,' he said, telling himself that he'd just earned himself an early beer.

'Hi,' Nancy Miller said, in a sing-songy voice as she welcomed Tim and Sandra at the door. 'Come in you two. Don's out back. Kids are upstairs.'

Tim smiled at her as he walked past her into the house. She sure looked good, he thought, suddenly feeling slightly less annoyed at being there. Nancy didn't have the cool grace Sandra possessed, but then Nancy was always so pleasant. So relaxed.

'Is that a new suit?' he asked her, looking her up and down, making sure it was in a way that would be considered neighborly. Her white bikini contrasted sharply against her honeyed skin.

'Yes,' Nancy sang, tilting her head this way and then that way, her long chestnut bangs threatening to pop out from behind her ears.

'I like it,' Sandra said, slipping her fingers behind the fabric covering Nancy's breast, feeling it between her thumb and fingers. 'It isn't lined,' she said, instead of saying what she meant.

Nancy laughed and stooped forward briefly, catching a lock of her hair and running it back behind her ear as she straightened up. 'No, it's not,' she said. 'I can't go into the water with this on, gets transparent in a second.' She laughed again, covering her mouth briefly. 'I found that out the hard way, once. But just once. Whew, did I give everyone at the pool a show!'

'Oh, that's too bad,' Tim found himself saying, gazing at her navel.

'Yeah, you wish you were there,' Sandra told him, giving him a whack on his behind before pushing past him and heading back through the house into the back yard.

Tim told Nancy to go on without him and ran upstairs quickly to check on the kids. Seeing them all playing nicely together for a change, he quietly popped back downstairs and met Don in the doorway of the kitchen.

'Tim, beer?'

'Yes, absolutely,' Tim said, leaning against the door frame and watching Don tower above his refrigerator as he opened the door with his hand on the top of the box. He removed four beers with one hand, a bottle neck between each finger, and handed two to Tim.

'Take two, they're small,' he said. He laughed loudly at his own joke before bringing a beer to his mouth and wrenching the cap off with his teeth. He spit the cap into the sink and then motioned Tim for them to go on outside. 'What's new?' he asked as they went. 'How's work?'

Tim walked in the darkness Don had created until they were out in the sunshine, following him over to the barbecue. As they stopped he tried to gauge where he would be safest standing, in case the thing were to suddenly teeter over right then and there.

'Yeah, everything's okay. Too much work, but then, you know. I go home when I want to. And you?'

Don set his other beer down on one of the shelves below the pit of the barbecue and poked at the flaming briquettes gently with a pair of tongs as Tim placed his own extra beer on the grass in the shade next to him. Don looked at Tim then. Tim watched his expression turn into a scowl, as if he had suddenly figured out what Tim was thinking.

'Ah, it's shit. Just shit. The boss is never there, and we know our results are coming out soon, and we're supposed to be reassuring the clients that we had a good year but we can never get any real information about how we're doing from the guys in accounting. I hate it, you know? Thinking one thing, and saying another thing? You know what I mean?'

Tim adopted a severe expression and found himself leaning on the barbecue, nodding his head. Then he quickly straightened up and crossed his arms over his chest, taking care not to lose his grip on his beer. He nodded some more.

'Yeah,' he said. 'Yep. Sucks, doesn't it?'

Just then the kids came storming out of the house into the backyard. Don's children, Tommy and Brigitte, raced up to Tim, each one grabbing a leg before they began swinging at each other, their giggles turning into angry cries as they used the barbecue as a barrier, each one trying to better the other at using it as a shield.

Suddenly, Tim grabbed both of them and pulled them away. 'Hey!' he shouted, 'You don't play around the barbecue, okay?' He looked at Don briefly as he realized that he had raised his voice a bit too much. Don watched him for a second before turning his attention to his children.

'That's right, how many times have I told you two?' he said. As he straightened up and took his place again at the barbecue and picked up the tongs, Tim's girl Monica climbed out of the sandbox with a piece of wood in her hands and began marching towards the barbecue. Tim saw her only after he had managed to get Tommy and Brigitte interested in the inflatable swimming pool and stood up quickly, his hands on his hips.

'Monica!' he screamed, checking to see that his son Ryan hadn't followed her out of the sandbox.

'The wood belongs to the grill,' she explained, not slowing down a bit as she came up behind Don.

Tim dashed over to her and placed himself between her and the barbecue, holding his arms out from his sides and crouching like a linebacker.

'No!' he said sharply. 'You aren't to come anywhere near the grill, you hear me? You stay away from it! Do you know what could happen to you if this barbecue fell down on you?'

'Tim!' Sandra called out. 'That's enough! You know Monica knows better. She won't do anything stupid.'

Tim began to stand up as he looked over to his wife, his hands grabbing the air in frustration at being contradicted when disciplining his own child. Sandra was always doing that. Always throwing her weight around. Tim was a nice enough guy to let her get away with that kind of thing.

As Sandra stared him down, Monica stepped forward until she was just inches from the barbecue and tossed the stick into the open area under the feet of the grill. Tim caught sight of her movement and turned to see her as she turned to go back to the sandbox.

'Monica!' he cried again, 'Didn't you hear me? You are not to go that close to the Goddamned barbecue, understand?' He watched Monica as she sulked back to the sandbox.

No one said a word. Tommy and Brigitte went back inside and stood looking out into the back yard at Tim.

'Tim,' Don called to him, holding the tongs out as though they would help him to explain himself. 'Hey, it's okay. Come over and drink your beer.'

Tim looked at Sandra, who would not return his attention. Nancy looked at her and put her hair back behind her ears.

'Hey,' Nancy said to her, 'you're getting really tan, aren't you?'

They had just come home from a weekend away and were busy unloading the car. Tim told Sandra he would finish up and was heading back out to the car under the darkening Sunday evening sky when he looked into the Millers' yard and stopped. The blinds were drawn. They must be away somewhere, too.

'Now's my chance!'

Tim hurried back to his front door and poked his head inside. 'Sand?'

'In here,' she called back from the living room.

'Gonna take the bike rack off the car, see if I can't fix it real quick.'

'Oh, Tim,' Sandra whined. 'Now? We just got home, and I'm starving. You said you'd cook tonight,' she reminded him. He took his head out from the doorway and stepped over to the palm tree near the mail box and gave it a good kick.

'Tim?'

Tim kicked the tree again and then leaped back to the door. 'Yes! I know I said I'd cook, and I'll do it! Just give me a minute! Eat some chips or something in the meantime,' he said as he closed the door behind him, just as he heard the television come on. Fuck, fuck, fuck! She always had to ruin things! But actually, this time it shouldn't matter. The barbecue would go down easily. He was sure of it. All he'd need to do was give it a good push... No, that probably wouldn't work. How long would it take? He remembered the television: good. Maybe she'd be tied up for a while and would leave him in peace. He stopped as he arrived at the wall and looked at the house again to make sure the Millers hadn't returned yet. With everything clear he jumped down into their yard and went to the grill. He approached slowly, sizing it up. Looking at the skinny base Don had built for the barbecue, Tim once more felt sure it would not take much. He took a few steps back and then lunged at it, jumping into the air, his right foot held high in a completely hopeless attempt at kung fu.

It hurt. And the barbecue was still standing.

Picking himself up off the ground, he grit his teeth and moved to the side of the grill, this time coming at it with his shoulder.

'Ow!' he groaned, wondering as he did how he could have failed to imagine how hard concrete could feel. Suddenly he realized that this would be a tougher job than he'd imagined. He had to start over. Devise a different plan.

Tools.

Of course. There weren't many other choices, outside of driving his Jeep through the hedges and ramming the thing, after all, but yes, he would need tools. He turned and sprinted across the small yard, vaulting up into his own and coming around his house to the front door. He stopped and opened it quietly.

Inside. Shut the door. Get downstairs to the cellar.

He stopped at the bottom of the cellar stairs and looked at the tools hanging against the wall. His eyes fell upon a medium-sized cold chisel he had bought long ago and had never used.

'Yeah.'

He stepped over and took it from the wall, then began searching for his big hammer. He found the little one right away, but the big one wasn't where it should have been. 'Shit. What the hell?' he said, backing up to take the entire wall in.

The big hammer was gone.

Tim bent over and was yanking on the tab of his toolbox that sat under the workbench on the floor when he remembered he'd lent his big hammer to Don some days ago. Oh, that's perfect! What am I going to do now, break into the house too? Wait a minute, didn't Don say he needed the hammer to straighten the barbecue tongs that he'd managed to step on? Well, something like that, anyway. Maybe the hammer is outside. It might even be near the barbecue. He bounded up the cellar stairs, stopping at the door on impulse to take the flashlight from where it hung on the wall, and was back in the Millers' yard again in seconds.

'Aha!' he cried, seizing the hammer that lay conveniently on the shelf of the grill. He got down on his knees, looking for what looked like a weak spot. Up close, the bricks and cement looked sturdier now, but the light was poor. He paused, taking a moment to imagine seeing himself in the act of what he was about to do. Do I really want to do this, he wondered. Of course, no one would suspect anything. It would look like an accident. It would look like what Tim had worried about happening had simply happened, and the darned thing had just fallen down. And then he'd make sure to help Don put it up right. Feeling the weight of the chisel in his hand, he took a deep breath.

'I'm *doing* this,' he said quietly.

He switched on the flashlight and ran his fingers along the left side of the wall that was only one brick deep, feeling for irregularities. Finding none, he did it again, pointing the flashlight beam on the brick as he ran his hand over it. This time he noticed a line of crumbling cement. A weak spot. Setting the flashlight down, it's beam falling on the glass door of the Millers' back yard, he scooted further to the side and placed the tip of the chisel on target, bringing the hammer back and letting go with a hard whack. As soon as he did, he felt the water on his back.

'What the hell?' he said, scrambling to his feet, wondering how hitting the grill like that could possibly spring a water leak on him before he realized that it was just rain. Only rain. He laughed to himself and let his shoulders drop.

'Oh, shit. Rain!' he spat, realizing at once that he of course didn't want to be doing this outside in the rain. He threw himself to the ground and began blasting away at the brick with the hammer and chisel, determined to get this mess over with so that he could get back inside.

Just then he heard her voice.

'Tim?'

No!

Tim quickly stepped over the Millers' back gate and quietly walked to his car that sat parked in their spot behind the house just a few yards away before answering. 'Yeah,' he said, barely able to make out Sandra's form through the tall hedge as she stood at the sliding door.

'It's raining.'

'Yes, thanks, I know. Look, I'm almost done. Just give me another minute.'

He waited for the silence that he would need to hear before rushing back to complete his job. Just as he thought it had been issued, he heard Sandra's voice again.

'You know,' she began, a scolding tone in her voice, 'if you had just taken that thing off like I told you to and not insisted on driving around with it on the car when we're not even using it, you wouldn't be out there right now in the rain! Why don't you just do what I tell you?'

Tim was spared the frustration of providing an answer to Sandra's unbearable prodding as he heard the glass door close and lock. He lowered his head and looked at the asphalt at his feet shimmering under the street lamps, and the drops of rain landing all around him as he felt the force of his will ebbing away from him, slipping out as if from a leaky balloon. Sandra. Why was she always right? And why couldn't he ever admit it until it was too late?

He looked up at the house. The curtain had been drawn over the sliding door. He looked at the bike rack and at the lock on one of the clamps that had been damaged when Sandra backed the car into a post. In a flash, he dashed back over to the Millers'. He got down on his knees and raised his head, listening for signs of anyone, or anything, before resuming his noisy task. With everything clear, he positioned his chisel and brought the hammer back.

Suddenly he stopped short. What if the thing falls on top of me, he thought. Realizing he had no way of knowing where the barbecue would fall, he hesitated as the chisel began to tremble against the red brick. He glanced around him, his eyes immediately finding the beam of light from the flashlight as it brought a shine from the handle of the Millers' sliding glass door. The shine turned into a kind of silvery gem as he let his eyes lose focus, once more questioning himself under the threat of his own extinction if the grill managed to fall in the wrong direction. As he watched the diamond glittering through the falling rain, a smile came to his lips, followed by a short laugh as he felt the thrill of disaster's teasing. Wiping the rain from his eyes, he grabbed the flashlight and turned it toward the brick. He brought the hammer back and gave it everything he had, the pinging of the hammer against the cold steel covering Sandra's urgent whispering for him. He stopped and felt the gaping hole he'd made in two of the bricks before taking up the hammer and chisel again and working in steady, determined blasts.

This is going to work. It *will*. It has to.

'Tim?'

He stopped, raising his head. Was it his own noise, or did he hear something?

'Tim!' a bewildered voice came from directly behind him. 'Tim, what are you doing!' Don Miller cried.

Disaster sneered as Tim turned around to stare through the storm at the figures huddled together behind him. Don and Nancy stood under an umbrella, with Sandra at their side under her own.

'We just got back,' Don explained, speaking woodenly, as if recounting a distant episode. 'I saw the flashlight pointed at the house. I thought it was a burglar. I went to your place and told Sandra to get you to come over. To help me look,' he said, his voice trailing off as his eyes began to pick out random objects in the yard before returning to his neighbor. Still on his knees, Tim turned to face them all squarely, resting his hands on his thighs, still clutching his hammer and chisel. He met Don's questioning gaze, then Nancy's, and finally Sandra's; the most difficult one to bear. As his resolve began to evaporate and he realized how crazy he must look in their eyes, he told himself that he would not resist Sandra's certain upbraiding. The thought of it didn't worry him as much as the thought that the barbecue still presented a threat to them all. As he raised one leg and planted his foot in front of him, placing his hands on his knee to stand, he heard a thumping crunch behind him.

He found himself on his rear a few feet from where he had been kneeling on the ground just moments before, his heart pounding furiously in his chest as his eyes beheld the mass of white cement laying before him in a fractured heap across the lawn. He glanced up at the others as Don Miller let out a shaky 'Jesus Christ!'

They were all okay.

Tim looked back at the fallen giant and smiled as he got to his feet and apologized to them all.

Nadya of the Soviet Union

Nadya sighed as she sat down in the seat near the back of the bus. No, take the window seat. That's better. Like being lost in a velvety indigo forest, she thought as she sank into the tall seat. My own little cell. No one can see me, and I can see no one else. All the better. She looked outside through the rain spattered window at the driver whose gnarled hands took one package after another from the waiting passengers and placed them - suitcases, wooden boxes, folding baby strollers, an automobile tire still mounted to its wheel which was not taken without some haggling - into the storage compartment on the side of the bus that occupied a space underneath the interior floor of the surprisingly shining Kamaz headed for Moscow. Nadya let her gaze move on to the gray sky above the equally gray city of Samara. Home to more than one million people just like her. Or maybe not so much like her, she would say. It had been the only thing she knew, growing up there. But it had not been easy. She rested her forehead lightly against the cool glass and closed her eyes before a yawn overcame her and knocked a notch off her consciousness. She felt heavy. Thick. It was too early to be up, but of course, one cannot dictate the bus schedule. The drive to Moscow would take ten hours. They would arrive at about four o'clock. Why did it have to leave at half-six in the morning? I would be perfectly happy arriving at six or seven, she thought. Counselor, I move that the bus schedule be struck down and replaced. Eight-thirty would be a much more convenient hour to depart. She smiled to herself at her little legal daydream. Having recently finished her university studies in law, she had developed a tendency to entertain case studies and legal maneuverings in her thoughts, even when they strayed into the commonplace: what pair of shoes to wear, the weather, the best songs to dance to. And now the bus schedule.

It was nice to smile.

But as soon as she had realised it, felt the pleasure in her face, the mood slipped away from her, and she was transported back to life. Her life.

She sighed again. She should have been filled with energy. Filled with excitement. She was really doing it! She was finally going to Moscow to live! All her life she had dreamed of doing it and now, having been accepted to the university in Moscow for some courses to add a specialisation to her field, she was going. Just like that. Papa would have been so proud, had he lived to see her off. As would her grandmama, and opa, and all of the cousins and all of her friends. Of all of them, she was the only one to be going to Moscow to live. Some had been able to go to travel, but none to live. Not one. And now she was going. It was something amazing. Something special.

But under these circumstances, only those closest to her were happy for her. The others were opposed to her leaving Bruno. To be leaving him 'all to himself,' some had said, as though he were a child in need of protection. In need of someone to look after him. They knew, of course. They all knew what he had done. But again, only those closest to Nadya had taken her side. 'It is in a man's nature to run away from time to time, before coming back to his woman,' others had said. 'He's a good man, but he's only a man! A man must have his fun. A man must have his pleasures,' they had told her. 'He must have been drunk, anyway,' they had added, as if that should remove him from his obligations. A woman lets her drunken lover run off with another woman because that's what men do. Well, not to me, she had told them. It won't do for me. Justice. Your honor, there must be justice. We must uphold decency. We must uphold honor, honesty, and trust.

And then there was the pain. The pain of being left alone for another. Even if only for a time. Even when he came crawling back. I loved you. I loved you, and you loved me. We told each other our secrets. We gave each other our hearts. We became one body and one soul and then you took my body with you, took my soul with you, and rubbed it all over another woman. How could you? How could you do that to me? She opened her eyes and looked outside. She thought she saw raindrops. She closed her eyes again. Leave me be. Just then the old song came to her and almost made her smile. The nursery rhyme that had meant more to her than to the other children.

> *What do you want, little girl Nadya?*
> *What do you need, little girl Nadya?*
> *I need nothing, just chocolate*
> *There is nothing I need, but some chocolate*

She tried to taste the chocolate as her face grew warm and her shoulders began to sag.

She lifted her head and opened her eyes as she felt a presence beside her. Someone had finally taken the seat on her right. A young man, she saw. She observed that he had not really noticed her, but instead merely sat, let out his breath slowly, let his head tip backward into the seat behind him and closed his eyes. Of course, Nadya had only glanced at him. She hadn't turned in her seat to face him. People didn't do that. It would have been considered nosey. But she was aware of this fact nonetheless. It was a fact. A fact that I would like now to submit as evidence, your honor, of the defendant's ignorance of the beauty of his seatmate. We can say nothing about his interest or lack thereof in the woman on his left. He was tired. Who wouldn't be at half-six on a Saturday morning? Also a fact: that the woman was indeed a beauty. A beauty, and an angel. A woman to be treated with the highest respect and devotion by anyone wishing to carry her heart in his hands for all eternity. Your honor, this I say to you.

She smiled again to herself. But she had forced it out. She felt no lightness. She felt only the faint pulling of an as yet unending panic somewhere deep inside. The panic born of the shock of a broken heart.

The bus driver closed the door. The diesel engine sent a shudder through the machine and then the series of undulations that would not cease for many hours began. The cool glass called to her. She closed her eyes once again.

Some had laughed at her. 'Love?' they had asked in astonishment. Love? What can it be? Who could care? In this world one cannot hold out for love. One cannot dream of it, even. We are born, we live, and we die. While we are here we struggle. We must struggle, in order to live. There is no other way. Love. Love? You must be joking. Stability. That is what you need. Food, clothing, a roof over your head. If you can achieve companionship with someone, if you can find a man and have enough with which to start a family, that is all one could ever ask for. Love is for lovebirds. You are not a bird, you are a woman. You need to start acting like one.

Your honor, I move that the world is indeed a cold and lonely place and that everyone has lost their minds.

Nadya opened her eyes, turned to the man sitting next to her and saw Bruno's face. A chill went down her spine and she felt her legs kick the seat in front of her. The man next to her stirred and opened his eyes.

But of course it was not Bruno.

He looked over at her but saw only the back of her head as she held her hand over her mouth and held her eyes shut tightly.

I must have been dozing, she thought. I must have drifted off. Who would blame me? Sitting in this bus so early on a Saturday morning, when most are fast asleep, recovering from their vodka and cigarettes.

Cigarettes. That's another thing I am happy to be leaving behind. The smell of cigarettes on his breath. I will not tolerate that again. Not for me. I will not turn a man away simply because he smokes, since most of them do. No. But I will insist that he stop smoking forever and always, once he realises that I am his queen and his goddess and that he cannot live without me. I will insist. There will not be any discussion. No further questions, your honor.

She gazed at the misty greenery surrounding the mountains that lay in the distance, to the north. So lush and green. If only there could have been bolts of morning sunlight splitting the sky, promising hope and warmth for all. Or at least for me. Bolts of golden light. A gift from the gods. I thought I knew beauty. I thought I saw it in the blue of his eyes. In the turn of his smiling lips, his chocolate brown hair, and his blue eyes. His ocean eyes, I used to call them. Oceans that I could escape into. Oceans that could take me anywhere on their rolling backs. Blue like the skies. There, in that blue, was space, air, light, time, peace, freedom, joy.

She curled her fingers into a fist. Stop it. Stop it now. And then, before she could stop it, she began to think of the child. The child that she had wanted to have with him. The child that she had dreamed of asking from him, when they could afford her. When it would be safe for her. Or him. It would not have mattered, for it would have been ours. Our child. With my lovely angel's face and his ocean eyes. She smiled, but could not prevent the burning from flooding into her face. Her cheeks grew hot and she needed air. She gasped, and felt the tears begin to flow from her eyes. Not again. Please, not again.

He had been staring straight ahead, unmoving, unblinking, as he fought off the loneliness that held him in its suffocating grip. Then he dropped his chin. No one should see me like this, he thought. He stared at his knees, then at his hands. He held them tightly in his lap. Then he relaxed them and exhaled, as if he could just will his worry to fly out of him and disappear into thin air, to find another victim. At least he was going home. Home, to his job and his friends and his cold and lonely apartment. Well. Things could be worse.

He turned at the sound of distress. What had it been? A whimper? The young woman sat next to him, her hands at her face, her face turned away from him. What had she seen? What was she looking at? Why couldn't I have been here earlier and been able to find a seat at the window myself? Easier said than done. Who can be on time - no - who can be *early* at half-six on a Saturday morning? Then he noticed her shaking. He became still. He opened his hands and placed his palms on his thighs. She was crying. He leaned slightly forward to get a better look. She turned just then and went into her bag for a handkerchief and looked at him. His heart sank. He saw her tear stained cheeks. He saw the pain in her face. Her beautiful face. God, there could be no sight more distressing on earth than that of a pretty girl crying. It was bad enough to see anyone cry. Even an old bum on the street, unshaven, haggard. He could not have it. He could not stand by to see it, for everyone became a child in his eyes when they wept. Everyone appeared to him to be nothing more than a mere child, alone and in a world far bigger and hostile than was right. It was as if he were god and they were his children. 'Oh, my dear one. Don't you cry. Don't you cry.'

But when it was a pretty girl, her pain leapt straight into his heart, and he felt the weight of her world pulling at his own.

He leaned forward, raising his hands slightly. He could not do nothing. 'Oh,' he heard himself say.

She wiped her eyes with the handkerchief she managed to pull from her bag and looked at him as he spoke. Oh no, how embarrassing. He was a ghost all morning and now he's seen me.

'Oh,' he said again, struggling to find the words. One needed just the right words in these cases. But he found none.

'Are you alright?' he asked her. Are you alright? Are you alright? Of course she isn't alright, you fool! Try again, and hurry. 'Please,' he heard himself saying, as he gave up all hope of finding just the right words. 'Please, don't cry.' He then smiled at her. It was an embarrassed smile. One that just slipped out without permission.

'Why not?' she asked him, suddenly realising that she was beyond the worst of it.

He saw what words were forming in his mind and didn't like them one bit, but did nothing to stop himself.

'Well, because then I'll start to cry too.' The young woman frowned. 'I'm sorry,' he said, 'but it's so difficult to watch you cry. Look, you've stopped now.' He smiled at her. 'I'm glad.' And then, before he could stop himself, 'Thank you.'

Nadya's frown pushed out a laugh at him. 'You're welcome.'

And then the both of them were smiling weakly. The difficulty had passed.

'It's a lovely view you have there,' he told her, motioning with his chin towards the mountains that went rolling by outside the bus. Nadya turned to admire the passing mounds of green and nodded.

'Yes,' she admitted. 'It's been some time since I've seen them.'

The man shifted in his seat, turning towards her. The errors of the moments before fell away from him. 'You've been to Moscow before?' he asked her. She is small, but not too small. She has a lovely hair color. She's dressed nicely, especially for someone from Samara.

She turned to him. 'No,' she admitted. 'This is my first time.'

He caught a touch of her fragrance as she settled round. She is lovely. Really lovely.

'And you?' she asked him.

'Oh, I live in Moscow.' He felt the familiar pride at those words as he spoke them, born of the fact that he had not originally come from Moscow. It was a different kind of pride from those who were truly from Moscow. A fawning pride.

She studied his face. Took in his overall appearance. Well, I should have known. I can see it now, of course. Definitely not from Samara. He's not bad looking, either. Sad eyes. He has sad eyes. Perhaps a bit thin. Thinner, certainly, than Bruno. Good then.

'Really?'

'Yes, in the Chystye Prudy. Do you know it?'

She thought for a moment. It sounded familiar. 'No, sorry. What is it?'

'It's a neighborhood in the city. A nice one, actually. I was very lucky to have found a place there, to be honest. But when I changed jobs...'

She is really very lovely.

She watched him expectantly. He seemed to have lost himself. When she was sure it was not something serious, she became amused. She raised her eyebrows. Tilted her head. 'Yes?'

'No, it's just...I was thinking.' Yes, you are a genius, now get going! 'When I changed jobs, they moved me there, actually, is how it happened. Just a lucky thing.' He stopped and glanced out the window. The mountains continued rolling by them. He looked at her and raised his hand. 'I'm Mischa.' She sat up to free her arm from between her ribcage and the seatback and took his hand. Soft hands. She has soft hands. Warm. Lovely. He continued without noticing it. 'Mischa, of the Soviet Union.'

He would not have known a thing had she not raised one eyebrow, had her lips not twisted into a very curious grin. But his words hung in the ether and were available for recall. What have I just said?

Why is he speaking English to me? He must really be in love with me now. 'Well. It's nice to meet you, Mischa of the Soviet Union. I am Nadya, also of the Soviet Union.' Now he is smiling again. Good, he is not a lunatic. Just a man.

His free hand went to his forehead. His other hand was no longer taking orders. 'Sorry, it's my job.'

'Your job?'

'Yes.' At the thought of his job he regained his composure. He released her hand and sat erect, gripping the elbow rest that separated them. 'You see, I work for the United Nations. In the International Transport Division. I'm always fielding calls from others within the organisation representing countries from all over the world, and it's common for us, you know, to identify ourselves that way.'

She nodded. 'Oh. And you speak English then. I see.'

'Yes. When I answer the phone.'

'But, you only used your given name.'

Mischa paused. She is bright. She notices details.

'Yes, well the Americans always do that.' Mischa knew that this would cause the girl to experience an envious thrill. 'And anyway, I like to be on a first name basis. It's nice, even though the organisation is so large that, well, it isn't like you speak to the same five people every day.'

Nadya shifted in her seat. This was serious. A stroke of good luck, and it wasn't even seven o'clock in the morning. 'Interesting,' she told him, making sure as not to appear more than politely impressed. She paused. Let him think that perhaps she would have nothing more to say about it. Let him start to wonder a bit. 'And what kind of education does one need for this type of work? Or did you know someone already? Perhaps a family member?' Naturally, one must assume that brilliance and hard work may not have been what brought him to his station. He must know that I am clever enough to be aware of this fact of the world.

'Well, I'm not sure,' he began, leading Nadya to begin to fear that perhaps he had merely been placed into this role through personal connections after all. That would have been most disappointing. 'For my part, I have a degree in international relations from Moscow University. But you have to realise that my department is rather small, and we generally do not have very much contact with others. I must admit that I don't know yet very much about what qualifications are relevant or required to do the kind of work I do.'

Nadya looked at his hands. They were nice and clean. Strong, but certainly not the hands of a brute. Not much hard work done in his life. She imagined what it would be like to hold his hand.

'What about you?' he asked her, breaking her concentration. 'What's taking you to Moscow?'

Now it is my turn to impress. 'I recently finished my legal studies in Samara and am going to Moscow University to take specialty courses,' she told him. As soon as the words were out of her mouth, to her surprise, the young man frowned. It was a private frown. A reaction to what he had heard from her that he did not actually wish her to witness. He had revealed himself by accident. She could see it in how he handled himself now. In how he tried to twist himself into some other direction. Without success. Finally he closed his eyes tightly and put his hands to his face. What now? What has gone wrong? Since when does my law degree fail to impress people who do more than spend their time stacking vodka bottles and flicking spent cigarettes into the street? Mister Mischa of the Soviet Union, this was made for you! For just your type! Was it the way I said it? Do I have something hanging out of my nose? What could it be?

It could not have been more than a moment or two, but it seemed like much longer to her.

'What is it?' she asked him, folding her arms over her chest and then immediately unfolding them so as not to appear as flummoxed as she was.

The man removed his hands from his face. 'Not another lawyer, are you?'

She saw his expression. It was clear that he was not making a joke.

This pushed her near the edge of civility. Her tone was approaching a sting. 'What do you mean, 'Another lawyer'?'

And then before she knew it, the man reached out and put his hands on hers, and her barbs retreated inside themselves.

'I'm sorry,' he told her. And this time with a very dear look in his eyes. 'It's just that everyone in my family is a lawyer!'

Nadya frowned. Then she gasped. 'Really?'

'Oh, how they were all so disappointed in me, that I chose to study business instead of 'The Law!"

Nadya laughed at his words. Wonderful. This isn't bad at all.

'I mean, you would think that they would have *liked* the idea of having someone at a family gathering who had a *different* story to tell, right?' Nadya nodded her agreement. 'Oh, I tell you,' he cried. Then he looked directly at her and leaned forward. 'My father, my uncle Vladimir, my father's father, my *mother's* father, *both* of my brothers. And, you will not believe it, but also my own dear mother is a lawyer. So you see... Pardon me if I act like a man possessed, but in this case it is true.'

Mischa sat holding Nadya's hands, and then he realised he was holding her hands. It was her own downward glance at them that gave it away. He was about to withdraw himself, to observe the rules of proper conduct, when she looked up again and into his eyes. His sad eyes that now shined. And then, like a kind of miracle, she closed her fingers around his hands. He could hardly breathe. Neither could she.

The two of them sat very still, drawn to each other by something neither of them would ever fathom, or would ever need to fathom.

Your honor, I move that this case be dismissed. Circumstances have changed dramatically since I began my opening arguments. I beg your forgiveness if I have in fact wasted your time, but I have learned something that changes everything.

Anoisia, America

Norm Gysin nearly collided into them as he entered the building of Anoisia Cross-Integrated Business Solutions where he had an appointment to see someone about a job that had been advertised in the local paper. If it weren't for the newspaper that he held carefully folded in front of him which touched the back of the person in front of him ever so slightly, he certainly would have. Would have bumped right into them. That would have been something his little sister Emily would have immediately seen as a "sign" that the day was off to a bad start and that he should under no circumstances proceed any further on that day with the job search. Luckily, he thought to himself, that's not the way he saw things.

He had just come in from the windy avenue, stepped out of the revolving door, and had glanced behind him just for a moment to see if in fact the leaves that had seemed to be following him since he had left the coffee shop were still following him, when there they were, half a dozen of them, their gloves and scarves not yet removed, standing together right inside the doorway gazing upward with their mouths open like a choir of mimes.

He stopped short and pulled his paper to his chest, looking up as he did at what was causing the traffic jam. A huge, television-like screen hung from the high marbled ceiling showing a colorful chart plotting a line that fought against the nooks and crannies to rise up, and up. What was that?

He was ready to shrug his shoulders and not give it another thought until he noticed the title of the chart and smiled sheepishly: 'Anoisia Stock Price.'

There it was again, the strange feeling he had at the word. Anoisia. What was it?

Although he was sure he had gone unnoticed by the television club in front of him, he felt the need to excuse himself, and did so quietly, to no one in particular. Of the small group before him, their young, eager eyes fixed on the chart overhead, only one paid him any mind. A woman. She noticed him, made eye contact, and smiled courteously before moving away from the others toward the rows of elevators to the left. Norm's foot took his impulse to follow the young woman seriously, but after making a few steps in the direction she had gone, as he watched her dark, chocolate-colored head disappear into a sea of people who certainly knew where they were going, Norm realized that he still had to figure out where his interviewer was if he was going to make something of this stab at employment.

He stopped and took in the sights around him: he was in the lobby of the Anoisia building. It seemed as busy to him as a train station. There were people everywhere. Norm looked at them. Most were smartly dressed, attractive, slim, and had a look on their faces as though they had just been handed instructions to diffuse a bomb and they couldn't wait to get their hands dirty. He had never seen so many confident, purposeful-looking people in one place in his life. Norm watched no one in particular and wondered if he belonged there. With this thought on his mind, he noticed that although the proliferation of people swarming around the place changed constantly, it never seemed to change.

'No,' Norm said pleasantly to himself, as he was inclined to do, 'that's just an equivocation.'

The interior was covered in marble, allowing sound to act as if it were in a veritable playground, free to skip and run and bounce off of every available surface. There were massive columns that rose up from the floor like giant redwoods, disappearing into the ceiling. To the right, far off in the distance in the corner, was a kind of lounge complete with a tended bar. The opulence of the place was phenomenal. Isn't this what bank headquarters looked like? Places where it made sense because you knew that they were filled with money? What kind of business was this Anoisia in, anyway? Norm knew it wasn't a bank. In front of him, some two hundred feet back, was a counter where two men dealt with a small army of people who obviously needed something from them. Norm squared his shoulders and set off for the front desk.

'Come on, Norm, if these rocket scientists can all get jobs here, then you should have no problem,' he told himself.

As he strode across the polished floor he took note of the squared jaw and the thinking lips of those all around him and tried in some small way to emulate them. Having crossed the expanse of stone he stood in line and held his empty briefcase nervously in his right hand before shifting it to his other hand and then back again, waiting for his turn to announce 'Which bomb is mine!' and then he noticed his shoes. Somewhere, he had managed to pick up a nice wet lump of mud that sat threateningly on the ridge of the sole of his wing-tip hand-me-downs. The embarrassment of being noticed bringing such unseemly material into this place of high importance made blood run to his face. He was so wrapped up in thoughts of how to diffuse his shoe that he hadn't heard the man.

'May I help you, sir? Hello?'

Norm looked up at once. The man was tall and seemed to speak to the entire building full of people when he addressed Norm, who stood just three feet from the desk now. 'Yes!' he cried. 'I'm ready.'

'Ready for what, sir?'

When he remembered what it was that he had come to the man for, Norm couldn't help but chuckle. The man before him softened just a notch. 'That's right,' Norm thought, 'laugh, and the whole world laughs with you.' Sometimes, he realized, as he had so many times in life, humor is the best plan of action. 'Oh,' he said, relieved to have found his feet again, and vaguely looking forward to his job interview. He laughed. 'Ready for the next bomb job.'

Sound doesn't just stop in a marble-coated lobby like that one. It's just not possible. Norm knew that, but it sure seemed right then to have grown awfully quiet, awfully fast.

'Bomb job?' the man hollered as his hand pulled a phone receiver to his ear with lightning speed.

They walked briskly in a tight mass, as though practicing football with the brakes on, and although Norm's own ears were filled with his own questions to himself that went unanswered he was sure he heard someone's whisper ricocheting off the marble, 'Is that him? Is that the bomb guy?' From his position in the center of the formation he strained to turn his head to see who had spoken, but could see nothing over the towering heads of his teammates.

They were very nice about it, actually, the men in the remarkably low-ceilinged rooms Norm had been whisked away to for questioning. As soon as they had passed him through a metal detector and searched through his things, as soon as he had explained himself over a cup of coffee, they told him they'd be happy to point him in the direction of Mr. Harper, the man he'd come to see about the job as a writer.

'Take the elevator outside up to the twelfth floor,' said a massive block of a man the others had called 'Kitty' who looked so severe that Norm wondered what expressions like 'Hold that bus,' might mean if spoken around him. 'Mr. Harper and the whole communications department are there.'

They were all smiles. Norm smiled too as he turned to thank them and waved over his shoulder as Kitty opened the door to let him out. He took a few steps down the hallway before risking a look back. He had to stop. Where was the door? What had happened to the door? He took a few steps back to where he had come from, his eyes roaming the fine wood paneling on the wall. He found a shy seam in the paneling, but no door. 'Well,' he thought, 'after all, it is the security department.'

The elevator traveled up through three underground floors before the buried-alive feeling left him and he breathed more easily. As he watched the twelfth floor approaching, he impulsively pressed a button and got out at the eleventh floor. Nothing like a tiny stroll and a visit to the men's room to freshen up before the meeting. He still had time, despite the detour. As the doors opened and he readied himself for inquisitive eyes and a rush of people, he was surprised to see nothing but yards and yards of cool, soft carpet. The chime of the elevator was an assault to such pristine surroundings, making Norm jump slightly as he stepped out of the car that quickly left him in total peace and quiet. There was no indication of the purpose of the floor, just the word 'eleven' in large brass letters on the opposite wall greeted him. To the right was a nook with two comfortable-looking chairs on either side of a coffee table on which sat the day's local paper before the hallway continued on a good distance and then disappeared around a left bend. The hallway to the left was a mirror image of the one on the right, but without the chairs or the table. It was nice. Oddly welcoming, yet without a living soul to be seen or heard. Norm glanced again at the newspaper, tempted to rest his bones and have a read. He looked at his watch: not really enough time for that. Better to just freshen up and then find the stairs to the twelfth floor.

He looked left again and saw a sign above a door in the hallway some ways down. He couldn't read the sign, as it lay flat against the wall, but imagined it could be a restroom. He set off towards the door until he could make it out: 'Women.' He looked further down and saw a similar door, also with a sign above it, and kept going.

'Men,' the sign said. It was clear enough. Norm pushed the door open and paused. The lights had been shut off. But a moment later there was a blink of light, and then he saw before him a perfectly inviting restroom. 'Oh,' he said, 'automatic lights.' Looking up and down the hallway, he stepped inside, and then smiled in mild embarrassment as he wondered to himself just why it was that he had looked up and down the hallway before entering the restroom. 'I'm such a funny man,' he whispered to himself.

He was like a kid in there. He immediately felt like testing everything in the room. What about hot water? Did the taps have hot water? He tried. 'Ahh,' he said, as the warm water fought off the memory of the weather outside. 'That's nice.'

Then, for no other reason than because it seemed like a good idea at the time, Norm picked up his briefcase and went into one of the stalls, which, to his delight, went from the floor to the ceiling. Inside, he hung up his jacket, took his coat off, and made himself comfortable.

No sooner had he done this when he heard the door to the bathroom open. Busy footsteps visited a stall on the other end of the row, followed by a loud shutting and locking of the door. As his neighbor continued to make things happen and get things done, Norm waited quietly for the peace to return to the room. Before he knew it, Norm's neighbor emerged from his stall and proceeded to use the sink to his full advantage. After one, two, three, four paper towels had been pulled and used and tossed, the steps once more found the door. As he expected to hear the door open, Norm was surprised to hear the footsteps cease instead. There was a click at the light switch, but the lights remained on. What's going on? Norm thought. Then the door swung open as another click was heard, this time casting the room and Norm into darkness. Norm's eyes opened widely. The steps vanished, and the door closed itself nicely.

Norm sat upright and put his hands on his thighs. 'What the hell!' he said. Then, wondering if the automatic setting had definitely been altered, he began waving his arms, leaning forward and backward, in a vain attempt to attract a sensor. It was still pitch black inside.

Norm sat quietly a moment and listened. Perhaps there was someone else coming? But he could hear nothing. Taking a deep breath he finished his business, stood up, flushed, hitched up his pants and put his coat and jacket on. He opened the stall and stood facing the blackness. It was really dark. He placed a hand out in front of him and inched forward, suddenly unsure how far the door was, or even exactly in which direction it was. He had made several small steps when the door once more swung open, leaving a man standing in silhouette before him. The man paused, then hit the lights. There was Norm, his hand outstretched like some kind of mummy making a break for it.

'Je-sus!' the man barked with a pronounced lisp, his elbows pitching outward sharply at his sides as if he'd just received an electric shock.

'The lights went off,' Norm said to him. But the man would have none of it. He gave Norm a nasty look as he passed him by and shut himself into a stall.

'What have I done?' Norm wanted to yell. 'What?' Norm looked at his watch: time to go. He opened the door and glanced at the panel of switches by the door. There were only two, with one clearly marked 'auto.' He looked up and down the hallway, knowing full well why he was doing it this time, before pressing one of the switches, bringing blackness once again to the room.

'Hey!' a voice cried from behind a closed door. Norm just grinned.

'Your turn.'

None of the magazines spread tantalizingly before him on the table, with titles like *Consult!* and *Wealth*, were at all appealing. For a brief instant he imagined that this was all a mistake, that he simply was not destined for a career in industry. His thoughts went to the applications he had recently sent off for doctorate programs at some of the top schools in the country. Perhaps the life of an academic really was the life for him. He looked at his watch. 'Well,' he thought, 'that could be. But I promised myself I'd take a stab at this life, and until I've given it my all, the jury is out.'

Confident again that he was doing the right thing, Norm took the extra moments to rehearse his speech that he planned to give to Mr. Harper, which went something like this: I'm interested in the job because I actually enjoy writing, and I can't imagine a better way to earn a living than to be paid for something that you enjoy doing. In that sense, I'd be a bit like a baseball player, or a rock star, I guess. I know I haven't worked since I finished my master's degree, but part of that has to do with the unfortunate incident I mentioned. I've been looking for this kind of work now for several months, but (and this was where he was stuck) I haven't found more than a couple of companies that seemed really interesting until now. Your company excites me.

He knew the last part sounded too puckery but it was the part he hated most about trying to get a job anyway, the part where you have to lavish praise on the company you are visiting to make them think something that they know you cannot possibly mean, which is that there is no other company that you want to work for but theirs. This dilemma was on his mind as he sat with head in hand, eyes focused on the floor before him, when two sharply polished black leather shoes appeared.

'Mr. Gysin?'

Norm looked up and then stood quickly, remembering as he did to provide an air of casual self-assurance combined with honesty, integrity and numerous other ingredients that no doubt came together to make him look like nothing more than a slightly nervous young man on a job interview.

'Ron Harper,' the man said, his hand coming up from his side like a switchblade knife, making Norm feel the impulse to jump – an impulse he was luckily able to overcome.

'Yes, Mr. Harper, glad to meet you,' Norm said, surprisingly smoothly, he thought to himself immediately, as he shook hands with his interviewer and proceeded to follow him down a wide corridor and into a large office space. Norm looked out over the desks of what could be, he imagined, his future colleagues. Many eyes watched him, curious to know who the new face was.

'This is my little department,' Mr. Harper said, waving his arm out over the space that held perhaps a dozen desks, all of them occupied. 'We're a small team,' he said, stopping to turn and hold Norm's complete attention. 'But let me tell you something,' he said, an air of hostility creeping into his voice. 'There isn't a single team here that works as hard as we do.' His eyes narrowed and Norm saw the blood creep into his forehead. 'We're *on game!*' he hissed, as if Norm had just cast a glance at his people and had said that they looked like the laziest bunch of turds he had ever seen.

'Exactly,' Norm said.

A moment later they were on their way again, Mr. Harper's mood having reversed direction, as he breezily jabbed his finger in the direction of the snack room, the coffee corner, and the room he called the 'Thought Distillery.' At the back of the space was Mr. Harper's office. It wasn't spacious, but big enough for his desk at one end and a sofa and coffee table at the other. Along one wall were windows looking out into the city. He led Norm inside, closed the door, and indicated where he should sit: a chair that sat in front of his desk.

'Not very cozy,' Norm thought to himself as he thanked Mr. Harper for the chair and did his best to pull it back as far as he could away from the desk without raising suspicion. Mr. Harper settled down and the two of them sat looking each other in the eye. Mr. Harper's eyebrow's suddenly popped up, as if he'd just asked Norm a question. Norm guessed the ball was in his court. He had to act.

'So,' Norm began, not at all sure what he would say next. Then he heard the words roll out of his mouth. 'How does it feel to be the head writer?'

Mr. Harper stared at Norm blankly for an instant before averting his gaze and swiveling in his chair, obviously having considered Norm's comment a bit of an insult. He rose, came out from behind his desk and began to pace the floor. Norm swiveled his own chair to follow Mr. Harper as he moved about in the small office.

'I'm not the head writer Norm, although I can see how someone like you, who doesn't at all understand just what it is that I do, could have that idea.' He stopped and raised a finger at Norm, a finger that he turned into a gun. 'Norm, I lead a swat team of carefully selected, highly trained professionals through the mine field that is corporate communications.' He pulled the trigger and then smiled as he resumed his aimless stroll. 'Yes, we have some writers, and yes, I used to be one of them, some years ago. The best, in fact. But now I'm a process man. That's what I'm all about.' His hands began a pantomime reminiscent of a Twister commercial. 'Processes and ladders and maps and... e-forces!'

'E-forces?' Norm said. 'Is that what you're into?'

'That's the name of the game, Gysin.' Mr. Harper had finished discussing himself and returned to his desk where he sat down and pulled Norm's resume from a file, looking at it slowly from the top down. 'Mathematics. And a minor in Greek and Latin! Fantastic,' he said, as if it were too good to be true. He continued to read quietly for a moment and then leaned back in his chair. 'Do you understand what it is that we do here at Anoisia, Norm?'

Norm knew this was a trick question, and knew that because he in fact didn't understand at all what it was that the company did to make money, he could very well be considered to be a fraud to be sitting there asking for work. It was apparent that Mr. Harper was content to wait patiently for an answer to his question. Norm felt the blood rising to his face and then remembered that he'd fingered through a copy of the company's corporate brochure while sitting in the security offices. He remembered a slogan at the top of the first page: We think for the world. It was the only thing he could remember. Norm decided to try to say a lot while saying very little. It was a gamble, but it seemed like his only hope other than admitting that he hadn't the faintest idea.

'The world needs a very good brain,' he offered, letting his words hang in the air as if he'd only completed half a thought and was extending it out to Mr. Harper for completion.

Mr. Harper smiled through narrowed eyes. 'Yes,' he said, 'well, I see you've done your homework, Norm. Very good.' He seemed then to accept Norm into his inner circle, releasing him from the lock of his gaze as he crossed his feet on his desktop and laced his fingers behind his head and stared out the window at the skyscrapers across the street. 'Gysin, our company is about giving advice to those in need of it. We're a pirate ship of ideas plundered from the various industries that we support, from manufacturing to Internet and e-business to civil engineering to financial institutions to, well, you name it. You name it, and we've got delta force in suits trained and ready to be out there, twenty-four seven, until the enemy is targeted and neutralized. Whether you're talking about open architecture, process-aligned solutions, or risk-transparent problem-process mapping systems, we're the ones.'

'Twenty-four seven,' Norm repeated.

Mr. Harper cast Norm a glance before his expression eased into a slight grin and his shoulders shrugged imperceptibly. 'Well, those are the foot soldiers, Norm. Not us. Of course,' he said, his expression quickly assuming a comical severity, as he snapped his feet off the desk and sat bolt upright, 'we're dedicated, dedicated to the cause. Those boys and girls in the fancy suits wouldn't last a day without us. We're their backbone.' He saw the alarm in Norm's eyes, and relaxed, taking a pen from his desk and examining it briefly. 'But we don't sit across the table from the client. We don't do all the traveling, and, we generally work reasonable hours.'

Norm was no closer to an understanding of what the company did than he had been before, and was not warming to the idea of working for the man who sat across from him, but he decided right then and there that until he found out what the actual job would be and how much they would be willing to pay him to do that job, he could not get up and say good-bye, as much as he felt inclined to do just that. Before he could help himself, he had blurted it out. 'What do you want me to do?' he asked Mr. Harper.

Mr. Harper was off and running as if he had known exactly that right at that very moment Norm would ask that very question. 'Gysin, our writing team has just lost one of its members. Defection to the competition. So we need a writer. But not just any writer, we need a writer who really knows how to use words.' He said it as if the suggestion were a bold innovation. 'We've got a lot of copy around here, in our corporate brochure, product brochures, plus speeches, presentations, you name it, and it all needs to be written in the voice of Anoisia, the voice of our business. It has to convey our core competence while carrying the stamp that is the innovation of our unique business guidance process. I've seen your samples, the ones you wrote while you were holed up in that mountain temple with your broken leg, or whatever it was, in China, you know,'

'It was India,' Norm said mechanically, wondering what writing Mr. Harper could have been referring to. What he had written while recovering from his injury in India last year was either philosophical or it was mathematical theory. But the writing samples he had submitted with his resume were from the bit of journalism he had done as a staffer on the college paper. Only the paper on organizational invariance theory, in which he had specifically mentioned having had breakthrough ideas while resting in the mountain hospital in India, came to mind. But he had sent that to Yale and Berkeley and... Or could he have switched the papers by accident and sent that paper to Anoisia? He must have. There was no other explanation for it. What a fool!

'India. Right,' Mr. Harper said. 'That stuff is remarkable. When I read it I saw immediately that you could be one of us.'

'Oh,' Norm said, still cursing himself at his error but perplexed at its reception. 'The one on organizational invariance?'

'Exactly! That was it.' Mr. Harper's eyes were alive. 'That's the voice of Anoisia! You've got it, my man, and it don't come easy. What do you say, will you join us?'

Norm was shocked. Was that all there was to it? Had he really just been offered the job? Was all the mental preparation paying off without him even having had to work up a sweat? 'Well, I guess I'll need to know at least a bit more,' he stammered.

'Ninety-five, starting. If you pull through the first six months, I'll guarantee you six figures. Come on, Gysin, you know this job was made for you.'

Norm was speechless. He had hardly hoped for half of the salary they were offering him. He briefly thought of the strategy to never accept a first offer, but immediately found it silly in this case. Holding out for more would be selfish. Arrogant. He had no idea what his job would be. How could he ask for more money?

'Give it a try. You can't lose,' Mr. Harper cajoled.

'Yes. My thoughts entirely,' Norm said, figuring that if he didn't like the job once he found out what it really was he could always quit. It was simple. There was no obligation for him. What could he lose? 'It's a deal.'

'Brilliant!' Mr. Harper shouted, taking Norm's hand and cranking it once, as though he were fixing a piece of farm equipment. 'There's no time to lose. Can you start tomorrow?'

'I don't see why not.'

'Winner. Be here at nine and I'll set you up. Sound good?'

Norm nodded and before he knew it he found himself back out in the windy streets. On the bus home, he thought about how he would go about discovering what his job was. Hopefully, he thought, it would just be obvious as he went through the motions of his first day. It would just become clear to him. He would learn who the other writers were, and watch them, talk to them. How complicated could it be, after all? He couldn't wait to tell Emily about his day.

'Ah,' Mr. Harper said, turning around as he did and leaving the attention of his team, assembled before him as they were for what could only have been some kind of meeting or announcement. 'Speak of the devil! Here he is right now.'

Norm had just ambled out of the elevator and stood in the doorway of number 1217 on the 12th floor of Anoisia Cross-Integrated Business Solutions. Mr. Harper glanced at his watch and shot a smile at Norm.

'And right on time, to boot. Anoisia likes attention to detail, Norm,' he said as he clapped a hand on Norm's shoulders, bringing a gritty smile to his lips. It wasn't the smooth start of his first day on the job that he had planned for, but, Norm thought, at least the introduction part would be over and done with soon. 'Everyone, this is Norm Gysin, the new writer.'

Norm renewed the strength of his smile and tried to clean it up a bit, dropping his chin slightly and then raising it again, wiping the slate clean. Mr. Harper's young-looking team of six produced in a mixture of smiles, nods and good-mornings that made Norm feel more or less at ease. He took a deep breath as he felt the sweat valves open under his wool suit and necktie and failed to stop his finger from plunging into his shirt just behind the knot of his tie and giving a firm tug.

Mr. Harper gave Norm an appraising look and then clapped his hands once before shooting Norm point blank with the imaginary pistols in each of his hands. 'Norm, tell my team what you're bringing us.'

'Well,' Norm began, his gaze lingering on Mr. Harper just long enough to ascertain if he truly expected him to justify his existence in the company to this group of strangers before he had even done so much as get a glimpse of his desk, to say nothing of setting his briefcase down and removing his coat. At this, Mr. Harper did not even give Norm the assistance of an encouraging nod, but instead narrowed his eyebrows, as if joining his team in waiting for a report on why indeed the company had seen fit to offer Norm a job.

But just as he was about to open his mouth to see what might come out in the form of an answer to the question, Mr. Harper spoke. 'Tell them the one about the organizational invariance, Norm,' he said, crossing his arms over his chest and grinning to himself, as if fighting to keep a secret.

'What on earth is this man's fixation with my academic writing?' Norm asked himself. The philosophical principle of organizational invariance held out little enough for the philosophers and scientists interested in consciousness and artificial intelligence that it was intended for, let alone this group of people working in communications for a consulting firm.

49

'Well,' Norm said, laughing out the word in three syllables like a game show host, feeling totally unsure of the wisdom of launching into a discussion on the topic. He glanced at Mr. Harper, whose expression had returned to one of curious anticipation. 'Oh God,' Norm thought, 'here goes.'

'Right. Organizational invariance is a theory holding that experience – and we are really talking about the experience known to conscious beings like ourselves – is invariant among systems sharing functional organization. Ultimately, the theory endorses the view that robots or synthetic humans could be created whose so-called 'experience' of their surroundings would not be qualitatively different from our own.'

Norm paused, lifting his eyes from the small point of nothing that existed between him and his audience that he typically concentrated on when discussing intellectually demanding theory, and tested the faces of his new colleagues.

No one spoke. No one smiled. A nod began to emerge from Mr. Harper. Almost imperceptible at first, it became amplified moments later until, before it became a distraction, a voice rang out.

' 'Functional organization,' ' a young man with the sleeves of his white shirt rolled up and his tie loosened, top button unbuttoned as though he'd already suffered through a long day, said to no one.

'Yeah,' said a plump brunette, her hair wound up and perched on top of her head like a small primate. She squinted at Norm through enormous eyeglasses. 'Cool.'

Suddenly the group was buzzing. Norm heard various elements of his little explanation repeated as heads nodded and hands gesticulated with no small amount of excitement. Norm found himself pulled into the group and before he knew it, he had shaken hands and exchanged personal greetings with everyone present.

He was part of the team.

'All right, all right,' Mr. Harper said, his annoyance not fooling anyone, 'Kathleen, Norm's yours today. Set him up, and ship him out. We've got our meeting on the annual report at eleven, and you all know that our Lord, Mr. Russell, will be there. This is,' he said, pausing and rolling his eyes as if he were speaking to a busload of idiots, 'an important day.' He clapped his hands and beamed a smile around the room that reminded everyone that he did, after all, love all of them. Every member of his small but dedicated team. 'So, I want all hands on deck and in the Thought Distillery at ten-thirty for a little jam session. We're not going to let those noodle necks in accounting steal the show today.' There was a brief silence. As everyone prepared to go on about their business, Mr. Harper's voice echoed once more. 'Gysin! You're in this one hundred percent today, you hear? See you at ten-thirty.'

Norm turned as a hand was laid upon his shoulder briefly. It was the brunette with the glasses.

'Hi,' she said. 'Like, I'm Kathleen.' She held up a waving hand and dipped her knees once in a kind of curtsy.

Norm remembered Mr. Harper's orders for his indoctrination and smiled at her. 'Oh, right,' he said, nodding. By now sweat was prancing freely down his back, making his eyes search for windows or air vents that might be put to good use. 'You know,' he said to Kathleen, his face showing a bit of agony for support, 'I've got to put my briefcase down and take my coat off, if you don't mind.'

'Oh, sure,' Kathleen said. With a wave of her hand she led him to a desk that stood just a few paces away in the back of three rows of two desks each. She switched on the computer before stepping back and allowing Norm access to his new station. 'Here you are,' she said. 'If you want something to drink, or, like, whatever, the coffee room's back there and the restroom is right next to it. Why don't you get comfortable and then let me know when you're, like, ready. I'll just go and get my computer booted up. I only just got here like a second before you did,' she explained, stepping over to the desk across the aisle from his and sitting down.

Norm looked towards the coffee room as if it were only a mirage, then set his briefcase down and took his coat off in a single, swift motion. '*Like*, okay,' he told her, smiling and hesitating to see if her excessive attention to the word 'like' was simply a joke played by a smart young professional writer, or not. But Kathleen simply stared at him, her mouth open. 'Thanks,' Norm continued. 'I'll do that.'

As soon as he had hung up his coat on the rack that stood between his and the next desk he headed straight for the restroom. Once inside, he stood in front of the sink and looked at himself in the mirror. Hardly the sweating wreck he had anticipated seeing staring back at him, he nevertheless was grateful to be able to wash his face with some cool water and look himself over. Especially since it seemed they had an important meeting to attend. The last thing he wanted was to screw up on his first day, even if it only involved looking haggard or having big sweat stains under his arms. After all, like they say, you never get a second chance to make a first impression. And hadn't Mr. Harper said that some big shot would be at this meeting?

Feeling in charge once more, Norm exited the restroom and followed his eyes into the coffee room, where he found one of his new colleagues standing before a drink machine. 'Hi,' Norm said, as his still nameless colleague turned to regard him before turning back to the machine without having said a word. A few loud bangs later, the young man bent down and retrieved a canned beverage from the pocket at the base of the machine. Standing upright again, he turned and looked at Norm with narrowing eyes. Norm recognized him then as the guy with his sleeves rolled up who had apparently been impressed with Norm's explanation of organizational invariance.

'I'm John, by the way.' Shooting a glance behind them through the glass into their workspace, he held the can up to Norm and let out a puff of air from his lips. 'Cheapskates,' he hissed. 'Make us pay for something to drink! What's next? Pay toilets?'

Norm felt it best to make a sympathetic gesture. He shrugged and shook his head as he raised his eyebrows once and exhaled sharply through his nose. Suddenly he had the impression he'd completely overdone it and fell silent, observing John's reaction. But he seemed not to have made a bad impression.

'Makes you think about empowerment and employee initiative transfer, doesn't it?' John said as he stepped around Norm and raised his head in a farewell gesture.

Norm wondered if he had heard correctly. '"Employee initiative transfer"?' he asked before helping himself to a cold can of sparkling water.

When he had returned to his desk, he took a seat and began reading the pop-up window on his computer screen. Of course. Password.

'Oh, there you are Norman.' It was Kathleen, rolling over on her chair with a grunt and a shove with her feet on the floor. She stopped just inches from the corner of Norm's desk before grabbing hold of it and wheeling herself next to him. 'I'm sorry, is it, like, 'Norman' or 'Norm'? I got your last name okay, but...' she said, trailing off so that Norm could supply the information she was looking for.

'Just 'Norm' is fine, thanks.'

'Right. Okay Norm, you need a password.'

Within minutes Kathleen had set Norm up with everything he needed to get logged on to his computer and covered the names, and much of the gossip, of everyone on the team. Norm nodded.

'Jay was the writer who just left us. Nice guy. Good writer, too,' Kathleen said, looking at Norm's computer screen with a private expression on her face. 'But I'm sure you'll be just as good,' she said, turning back to Norm and giving him an encouraging smile. 'Oh,' she said, 'by the way, I'm, like, the computer whiz, desktop publisher, marketing chick,' she said, patting Norm on the arm and then bringing a hand to her mouth quickly and showing him the palm of her hand in apology.

Norm just smiled. 'Well, thanks for the help,' he told her, glad to have a normal person sitting next to him. He looked at the time on his screen and checked his watch. The computer was right: ten-thirty. Just then he heard a shuffle of noise and looked up to see people rising from their desks and heading his way.

'Meeting time!' Kathleen told him as she turned in her chair and waited for Norm to react. She stood as soon as he did. 'This way,' she told him, falling in behind Peter, who brought up the rear of the team as they all filed into the Thought Distillery.

'Hey,' Norm whispered as he and Kathleen made their way to the room. 'Why is it called the 'Thought Distillery'?'

'Later,' Kathleen shot back, looking straight ahead.

The two of them stepped into the room, which looked like many meeting rooms, with a large oval table, an overhead projector in the corner that probably hadn't been used in ages, a flip chart in the opposite corner with notes scrawled on it from some previous session, a small table with a telephone. Kathleen and Norm took the last two seats available. Norm sat at one end of the table, noticing at once with a small amount of trepidation that Mr. Harper occupied the opposite end.

With everyone settled, the room became strangely quiet. Norm went from face to face and saw that the others had bowed their heads ever so slightly, almost as if in prayer, and seemed to be doing their best to be absolutely still and silent. He looked at Mr. Harper. Mr. Harper's eyes were nearly closed as he sat with both hands flat on the table in front of him.

Without warning, Mr. Harper inhaled audibly and opened his eyes, looking up as he did in a movement that was followed by the others. 'Ready,' he said, not asking. His voice was calm, but precise. Thoughtful, like a priest, or a psychiatrist. He turned to the young man seated to his right. 'Peter.'

Peter sat quietly, his gaze returning Mr. Harper's. 'Flexibility,' Peter said evenly. 'Flexible... solutions. No, flexible direction.' The last word was spoken with a mild emphasis, as if he had been particularly pleased with it, and yet, his contribution had been made in the same calm, even tone as Mr. Harper's.

A faint murmur issued from the others as Mr. Harper nodded once. 'I like that, Peter. Good start. Jennifer.'

Jennifer smiled ever so faintly. Was she nervous? She looked directly at Mr. Harper for some time. Neither one said a word. Norm felt the grip of his sense of humor tightening on him like a python, threatening disaster. It had occurred to him that Jennifer and Mr. Harper were engaged in a staring match. 'Oh no, don't laugh,' he told himself. 'Breathe deeply. Your turn is coming!' This last thought served to instantly squelch his rising instability, relieving his anxiety and returning him to the mere concern that he might be expected to participate in this game that hadn't been explained to him. As he began to be consumed with that unpleasant thought, Jennifer spoke. 'The power of thought.'

Mr. Harper's head adopted a nearly unnoticeable tilt. ' 'The power of thought,' ' he repeated. 'Okay. Very plain language, Jennifer. And not very original.'

'Yes,' Jennifer apologized, unable to hide a flash of disappointment in herself that flickered across her face and then was gone.

'But okay,' Mr. Harper continued, the corners of his mouth curling faintly, 'Okay. Think Anoisia, Jennifer. Remember Anoisia. John.'

There it was again, Norm thought. What was it about that word? There was something familiar about it, but what?

The process continued, from John to Kathleen, with Norm next in line. John's offering had been 'functional derivative lines,' and had gone over very well with everyone. Kathleen's suggestion, 'liquefaction knowledge base,' brought audible semi-gasps from the others, with one or two of them even managing to lose their composure and turn their heads away from Mr. Harper, just for an instant, to congratulate her with their eyes. Mr. Harper, for his part, leaned slightly forward after the commotion from Kathleen's contribution died down. 'Explain,' he said simply.

'Liquefaction,' Kathleen began, 'primarily from geological applications, to make or become liquid. I'm combining the notion of movement from this with 'knowledge base,' implying a proactive, dynamic consultancy.'

As the last word slipped from her lips and dissolved, the silence was palpable. Mr. Harper's expression remained secretive until his eyes glittered and he inhaled sharply. 'Marvelous,' he said. 'I see where you're coming from, Kathleen. It's perfect: 'Our people are on their toes, looking for solutions for our clients.' Kathleen, *winner*,' he said, allowing himself to beam for an instant before facing Norm squarely.

Norm watched his new colleagues break protocol as they all turned to look at the new guy for an instant before remembering that they were, in fact, in the Thought Distillery. Norm met Mr. Harper's gaze and smiled meekly. 'I'm not clear on what we're doing,' he apologized.

'What is it that you *think* we're doing, Norm?'

'Well, it seems you're trying to come up with buzzwords.'

Mr. Harper's face darkened. ' 'Buzzwords'? Is that what you think this is? Norm, these are more than just words. Think about it: what is this firm about? Solutions! Pure and simple. Well, we are *building* solutions right here and now. We, the comms team! These 'words' are taken by our consultants in order to fashion value for our clients and our company. We are building the product! Right here!' he smiled, spreading his hands out to indicate the group of people before him.

'Okay,' Norm conceded, preferring to keep his own opinion to himself for the moment.

'But I know it's not easy,' Mr. Harper said. 'Next time, Norm. Next time, we'll source your solutions, okay?'

'Right,' Norm said, forcing a smile to his lips as he nodded once.

When they had gone once around the table Mr. Harper and the others relaxed and appeared to become their normal selves. Kathleen received several complements from the others on her bit before Mr. Harper addressed the group again. 'Okay, people, we're about to go into a biggie, as you all know. Our new CEO will no doubt be paying careful attention to us here. The annual results report is nearly complete, as is our input on it. The main issue here is the new CEO himself. We don't know as much about Russell as we'd like. I know that. We don't know how he'll react to what we've put together.' Mr. Harper stopped as he noticed Norm. 'Kathleen,' he said, 'brief Norm on the way up, will you?'

Kathleen nodded and glanced quickly at Norm and smiled at him before returning her attention to her boss.

'I know it was easier, under Hegel, to feel confident that our work was appreciated for being one of the drivers of Anoisia's success, but I don't want any of you to worry. Russell has been in the consulting business longer than any of us. I'm sure he can appreciate the importance of effective communication in our new process-driven economy. I'm sure he will embrace our bi-directional, cross-platform, total open system empowerment process!'

A ripple of excitement coursed through the team at Mr. Harper's final comment. Glancing at the clock on the wall before standing and nodding to the group, Mr. Harper looked satisfied. 'All right team, we've got five minutes to ready ourselves and get upstairs. Let's go.'

When they had all filed out of the room and returned to their desks, Norm shot a glance back in the direction of Mr. Harper's office and then rolled his chair across the gap between their desks to Kathleen. 'Kathleen,' he began anxiously, 'What is going on? I don't understand what happened back there. And this meeting, I hope I'm not supposed to be involved in it. Are we really meeting with the CEO of the company?'

Kathleen held her hands up, palms out, and smiled at him reassuringly. 'Whoa, Nellie. Like, calm down. First things first. Norm,' Kathleen said, pausing to consider him carefully, 'frankly, I'm, like, a little surprised. You were hired because of that great writing you did. Come on, you know what our company is about, right?' Norm was about to say that in fact he did not, but Kathleen kept on talking. 'Consultancy is about knowledge transfer. That's all. In that room back there we cook up tools for communicating exactly what it is that we can offer to our clients. And it's got to sound good. Like, professional. Our direction in communication lies in the examples you heard in that room,' she said, tossing her head in the direction of the Thought Distillery. 'And your writing fits it perfectly. So don't worry. All you have to do is think about that writing. Think, like, organizational invariance,' she said, giving Norm an encouraging pat on the shoulder.

Just then Norm heard a door slam in behind them. Mr. Harper had emerged from his office and came marching up through the center of the room looking determined and ready. Immediately, the others stood up, grabbing notebooks, files, and other items they would need as they fell in behind him. Kathleen grabbed a thin leather zippered folder and flashed wide eyes at Norm as she stood up. Norm's eyes searched his desk, seizing hold of a pad of paper and a pencil that he quickly snatched up as the two of them set off for the others.

'Now, about this meeting,' Kathleen said as they all headed out into the hallway toward the elevator, 'Like Mr. Harper said, we have a new CEO, Burt Russell. Joined about a month ago. The company has been preparing its annual results. Our team is, like, a big part of that. This is our first meeting with Mr. Russell. We've just finished the primary layout for the report and are just going to like, go over it with Mr. Russell. That's all.'

Without missing a step the two of them joined the others in the elevator, taking the front position just behind the doors. For a moment, everyone stood quietly until they realized they weren't going anywhere.

'Norm,' Mr. Harper called from the back of the elevator, 'Can you hit the 37th floor, please?'

Norm looked to his left at the extensive row of buttons on the wall. 'Thirty-seven,' he said, his eyes searching the number out. 'Right,' he said, pressing what he had found and turning his head slightly as he did to make brief eye contact with Mr. Harper. Just then, Kathleen continued her debriefing in a near whisper.

'The main thing is,' she began, 'we don't know Mr. Russell's style of communication. You see, our current style was, like, developed under the last CEO and founder of the company, Bill Hegel. Actually, he like totally masterminded the whole method of communication used in the industry worldwide today.'

'But what will I have to do?' Norm asked.

'Nothing, don't worry. Take notes. Try to just like... *absorb*.'

With that, the elevator chimed and the doors rumbled open. Norm stepped out of the elevator. Behind him, the others came and they all began to flow into the hallway until Kathleen stopped. 'Wait,' she said, a puzzled look on her face. 'We're wrong here.'

Feeling the responsibility of their whereabouts shifting onto his shoulders, Norm's eyes fell on the brass number on the wall just next to him. Thirty-six.

'Sorry everyone, wrong floor,' Kathleen said, as they all turned and shuffled back into the elevator.

'Sorry,' Norm said, entering the elevator last, watching as Kathleen pressed the right button and wondering to himself how on earth he had failed in his first assignment yet on his first day on the job.

'Norm,' came Mr. Harper's voice, once more from the rear of the elevator, 'I thought you were an expert in numbers.'

The team broke out in relieving laughter, Mr. Harper included. Norm shrugged and did his best to suffer invisibly.

'I bet you did that on purpose Norm, didn't you? Break the tension a bit?' Mr. Harper asked him. 'Brilliant. Nice work,' he said, clearly pleased with the young man he had encouraged the company to place its faith into.

Norm glanced at Kathleen, who smiled and moved her elbow out, as if to offer him a congratulatory nudge. Before he could react, the chime sounded and the doors opened once more, this time revealing a darkly wooded corridor and a large doorway behind which an identical corridor stretched, with heavy wood doors dotting its sides, all of them closed. Norm exited the elevator and stepped to the side, waiting for the others to lead the way before falling in behind, with Kathleen dutifully waiting for him. They proceeded to the end of the hall and turned left. The door there stood open, allowing them to enter without breaking stride.

Norm's eyes went wide as he stepped into an enormous, sunny room, an entire wall of which was glass from floor to ceiling, revealing an impressive view out over the city. A collection of curved tables stood together forming an oval with room for perhaps forty people. Half of the chairs were already occupied. The nods and brief vocal exchanges of the others served to remind Norm of his lack of familiarity with his surroundings, but also managed to afford him a comforting anonymity.

'We sit over here,' Norm heard Kathleen say to him, pointing to the left. He followed his team to their place just right of the center of the formation and took his seat beside Kathleen, setting his pad of paper down and picking up his draft copy of Anoisia's annual report that sat neatly on the table before him. Flipping through it automatically, he tried to imagine that he could have any reason to be there amongst the others in this seat of power at the top of their building. He closed the report and let his eyes wander. Most of the people there were young, in their twenties and thirties, with few exceptions. They all looked to be at ease, or even slightly annoyed to be there in this wondrous room, taking precious time from the work that must have awaited them on some other floor of the building. He found himself smiling when he sensed Kathleen leaning over to him.

'Everyone's here,' she said. 'Finance, controlling, accounting, legal... you name it.'

Norm noticed a gentle squelching of conversation and followed the eyes of the woman across from him to the door, as four older men entered. The doors were closed behind them as they took their places opposite Norm, in the middle of the formation.

'All right,' one of them said, unzipping his leather folder and removing a pen from it before standing up and placing his fingertips on the smooth mahogany surface of the table before him. 'Since I'm sure some of you have no idea what your new CEO looks like, I'll just introduce myself now so that you all know who gets the highest interrupting privileges.' The man smiled at the group, and joined in their apprehensive laughter. 'My name is Burt Russell, your new CEO here at Anoisia-' He paused for just a moment and glanced at the man seated on his left, grinning at him momentarily before continuing. 'Cross-Integrated Business Solutions, yes. I've met many of you here, and you'll no doubt remember me. Others of you whom I haven't yet had the pleasure of meeting, please quickly introduce yourselves now by telling me your name and the department you work in.'

Uh oh, participation. Norm watched as Mr. Russell, still standing, raised his eyebrows and smiled, once more inviting those he had indicated to speak up. Moments later, after a brief throat clearing, a hand was raised until Mr. Russell's eyes had found it. Norm leaned forward to see who had had the courage to go first.

'John Parker, Mr. Russell. Group Finance, West Coast Region. Pleasure to meet you.'

Mr. Russell closed his eyes briefly and nodded. 'Mr. Parker,' he said.

As others volunteered to reveal their identities, Norm found himself caught in a game, telling himself he would not wait to be the last to speak up, therefore looking like he was afraid to manage such a simple task, while realizing that he of course had no idea how many others sat waiting to introduce themselves. What should he say, anyway? And should he also throw in a 'pleased to meet you,' or should he go for something more daring, perhaps something like 'I'm looking forward to your doing great things with us here at

Anoisia'? Or perhaps it was understood that the number of words one was allowed to speak at this particular opportunity corresponded to the length of employment one had seen in the company? In that case, he would only be entitled to state his name and his department.

As he struggled to find a suitable plan, he looked across the table again at the woman he had seen before. This time, as he watched her sitting there, her hands folded neatly on a small stack of paper before her, her eyes smiling at him just like they did the first time he saw her, her chocolate-colored hair now hanging down in a neat pony-tail, he recognized her. When he realized that she had recognized him too, he smiled hello to her before suddenly noticing that no one had spoken for a few moments, a gap slightly longer than had occurred as the others had volunteered, one after the other. Fearing that he was now the last and might lose his turn, he hastily spoke up.

'Hello,' he said, turning his head as he spoke to make eye contact with the chief executive officer, his hand shooting up and then returning just as quickly to the table with an audible thump against the hard wood that Norm would later curse himself over, 'Yes, Norm Gysin here...'

And then, with the force of his breath in his throat waiting to proceed, Norm realized that he did not know the name of his department.

As Mr. Russell waited, his eyebrows taking a small jump higher as he leaned very slightly forward in anticipation of his revelation, Norm finally recalled what Kathleen before him had said. 'Group Internal Communications,' he said, his hands turning into fists underneath the surface of the table.

Mr. Russell again nodded, his eyelids dipping once. 'Mr. Gysin, welcome to Anoisia,' he said, his smile lingering along with his gaze upon Norm as he correctly guessed at the cause of Norm's hesitation. 'Thank you all very much for coming,' Mr. Russell continued. 'We're here today so that you can hear my comments and answer the questions I have about the annual report. I've had time to review it, and while I find it acceptable overall, there are still some remaining issues. So, let's get to work. First, I'd like to hear from accounting.'

The sound of shuffling paper smothered Norm's anxiety as the men and women assembled around him began to get down to business. Norm caught a polite smile from the woman across from him and watched as her expression turned to one of regret. As she leaned forward, her eyes still upon him, he had an odd feeling that she was about to speak to him in front of everyone.

'Yes, Mr. Russell,' the woman began, turning to speak directly to the CEO. 'We're on track for our deadline and don't foresee any complications,' she said, before shifting her gaze to a group of gentlemen at the far end of the table, 'as long as HQ Finance meets their own deadlines regarding their 'special vehicles.' '

Norm thought he heard a shift in tone at the last phrase when the woman spoke. His feeling was confirmed when he saw her return her attention to the report in front of her, her eyes opening wider as if she expected trouble.

'Burt, Mr. Seemore's assistant here might not have the clearest understanding of just what it is that we're doing,' one of the men said, his hostility checked but obvious nonetheless. 'If he were here himself today he surely would not have bothered to shine the spotlight on us.'

'Well James, are you on schedule or aren't you?' Mr. Russell asked him, clearly uninterested in the politics of the situation.

'We are very much on schedule.'

'Fine. Do you have anything else to add, James?'

'No.'

'Good. Next stop, Controlling. Andrew, your side please?'

Norm watched as a balding man with small wire rimmed glasses jerked as he heard his name called, and wiped the sweat from his brow.

'Mr. Russell, sir, we've... we've nothing special to report. As you know, our work will really start as soon as the news, or,' he said, catching himself, 'as soon as our results are made known.'

Mr. Russell's eyes narrowed on a spot in the middle of the table as he absorbed the other man's comment. 'Are you sure, Andrew?' he asked him.

The man in the glasses mouthed something inaudible as he struggled to find his feet. He wiped his forehead with a handkerchief he had suddenly produced and breathed deeply. 'Like you, Mr. Russell,' he said weakly, 'I can only wait for the results to be calculated. I trust the people in Group Accounting and Finance to do their jobs, as they have in the past.'

'Fair enough then,' Mr. Russell said. 'If no one else has anything, I'd like to move on to your team, Ron. I've got some questions for you.'

Norm stiffened, startled as Mr. Harper drew in a sharp breath through his nose.

'Yes Burt, fire away!' Mr. Harper said.

'First of all, does anyone have any comments on the opening portions of the report – the letter to the shareholders or the year in review?' Mr. Russell's eyes traveled around the table once briefly. 'No? Okay, well I do. Of course, we don't have any final results yet, but we do know – and please, Shannon, correct me if I'm wrong here,' Mr. Russell joked to the young woman across from Norm, 'We do know that we've had a less than stellar year, right? The entire industry has been hit by the lack of confidence in the global economy since the stock market trashing we saw in the summer, and we know we're not any different. So why do I see this caption across the top of the letter to the shareholders: 'Seeking solutions, from strength to strength'? I mean, what does that even mean, first of all? Can you clue me in on that Ron, please?'

The luster in Mr. Harper's eyes had lost some of its shine, as Norm felt the heat run off his boss and onto the whole team. 'What it means?' Mr. Harper asked.

'Yes, exactly. I mean, 'solutions,' okay, another buzzword that I don't exactly like, but fine. But what about 'from strength to strength'? I know what that means, obviously, but if this is referring to events of the year, and it should be, then what specific events are you calling strong?'

'Well,' Mr. Harper began, his face turning pale, 'I'm sure that we...' He stopped as his eyes sought someone out in the room and went wide for a moment as they found him. 'Jack, didn't your European sales team take down a winner client with that mandate you sourced in France?'

A tall man with hair that was so black it was blue straightened up and shot a smile at Mr. Harper. 'Yes, we sure did,' he said, checking the reaction of the new CEO to this small bit of advertising for his team. Mr. Russell showed the palms of his hands to the group.

'Wait a second here, Ron. I'm sure we can point to successes here this year, some anyway, of course. But the *year* cannot be characterized this way.' And then, Norm's boss felt a stake being driven through his heart at what came next. 'We need to tell it like it is.'

Norm watched out of the corner of his eye as his boss wilted, a hand going to feel the stubble on his chin as he reeled under the revelation that their new CEO, Burt Russell, had no clue about effective communication in a cross continent, solutions-based new global economy.

'I see what you mean,' Mr. Harper said, buying time while he rushed to consider a solution to his dilemma.

'Now, before we leave this room, let's all of us put our heads together and come up with an appropriate kick-off for this letter,' Mr. Russell said.

Mr. Harper nearly fell out of his chair. All of us? What on earth was the new CEO doing, he thought, sourcing contributions to the crafting of messages from people from accounting? From finance? From *sales*, for God's sake? Running his hand through his hair, Mr. Harper picked up the glass of water that sat before him and had a drink. He was just about to suggest to Mr. Russell that he be allowed to take his team into the Thought Distillery for a quick response session when he noticed something to his left and turned to see Norm's hand rising hesitantly. As he fought the urge to reach out and knock Norm's hand back down where it belonged, Norm spoke.

'Sir?' he asked, speaking to Mr. Russell.

'Norm, yes. Got an idea? Let's hear it.'

Mr. Harper held his breath, hoping that the time Norm spent in the Indian hospital was about to pay off.

'Well, I don't know how bad a year we had, but how about this: 'Back to basics – our response to a tough year'?'

Mr. Harper winced as the words escaped Norm's lips. He smiled broadly to no one, his neck allowing his head to tilt and doddle like one of those plastic dogs in the back window of a car, his breath starting to come and go as if he were about to vomit as he prepared to apologize for his new employee's lack of exposure to Anoisia.

But before he could, Mr. Russell extended his arm over the table and pointed his finger directly at Norm. 'Now, *that's* what I'm talking about. Done.' He looked around the room as the nods and murmurs began to grow. 'Perfect,' he added. 'We're going to tell our shareholders how we at Anoisia are going to deal with the tough environment we're in that's going to make them all feel better about the future.' He snapped his fingers. 'Exactly,' he said. 'When did you join, Norm?'

'Yesterday,' Norm told him.

Mr. Russell looked at Mr. Harper and raised his eyebrows. 'Nice going, Ron. Way to go.'

'Yes,' Mr. Harper said, smiling weakly and nodding as he struggled to come up with something more to say.

With that issue out of the way, the meeting was adjourned. As everyone began rising from the table, Norm stood up and made his way along with the others from his team to the door. A head in front of him turned and spoke to him. It was his boss, Mr. Harper.

'Norm, after lunch I'd like to see you in my office.'

'Sure,' Norm told him. As he tried to figure out if the request would lead to something pleasant, or if it would turn out to be a headache, he felt a presence at his shoulder and turned to see what was coming next.

'It's Norm, right?'

It was the woman who had sat across from him. The one who was apparently the assistant of the man in charge of accounting. The one he had nearly bumped into on that first day.

'Right,' Norm answered. He found himself in the wide hallway walking slowly along with Shannon Parsons. Before he knew it, he had accepted her offer to go with her straight to lunch. They lunched together after that nearly every day.

A month later, Anoisia Cross-Integrated Business Solutions was the darling of the industry and of the global investment community, having managed to pull off a profit increase of more than ten percent when other companies were struggling just to stay in business. Anoisia stock was trading at an all-time high and outperforming the market handily. Everyone was flying high at Anoisia. Complete strangers greeted each other in the sunny hallways, trading giddy smiles and waves like old friends who'd promised to keep a secret that they were just dying to spill. The excitement rippled through the air like static electricity.

The annual results had been announced almost two weeks before, although most employees hadn't yet received their personal copy of the report. As a member of the team behind the report, Norm found a copy on his desk the day before. Now he sat at his desk over his morning coffee, thumbing through the report. He'd glanced through it briefly already, mainly to check to see if the heading for the letter to the shareholders that he had created was really there. Despite Anoisia's stellar performance, they had decided to keep it since their profits had not in fact reached the levels they had predicted at the beginning of the year. They also didn't mind the irony of their 'tough' year rubbing salt in the wounds of their competitors. Norm hadn't read an annual report in his life and probably wouldn't have had he landed a different job. But it wasn't that bad. After a few minutes he even found himself mildly entertained. The numbers were something for him anyway, being a mathematician. Having looked over the opening remarks, he flipped through to the income statement and balance sheet. Used to reading academic texts and journals where footnotes and endnotes were vital, Norm naturally looked up and read through the healthy sprinkling of notes that filled the pages. There he noticed that several companies had been set up during the past year in the Bahamas whose purpose was not at all clear. Norm found the contact information at the back of the report for all Anoisia offices and Group companies and rang up one of the Bahamian locations to ask them what they did. Were they just acting as consultants to companies on those islands, or were they doing something completely different?

The phone didn't ring more than a few times before it was picked up.

'Marshall Services,' the voice on the other end droned lazily, 'May I help you?'

'Yes, I'm calling from Anoisia headquarters in Chicago,' Norm informed the woman, 'I'm sorry, I thought I dialed Anoisia Bahamas.'

The woman sighed. 'You did. Marshall Services handles all calls for the Anoisia people.'

'Oh, I see. Well, could you please put me through to the person in charge of communications there please?'

'There is no one in charge of communications,' the woman told Norm as if he were a fool for asking for such a person. Norm didn't let her attitude bother him and remained friendly as he tried a different route.

'Well then let me speak to someone in sales, or better yet, one of the consultants. Any one of them, I don't care who it is.'

'Sir, there's no one there, do you understand?'

Norm let himself fall back in his chair. No, he did not understand. The woman said that Anoisia Bahamas is there, but that there is no one there! What kind of sense did that make? Then he realized that it might indeed be only a very small office. Maybe they were at lunch, or on vacation? 'Oh, I see,' Norm replied. 'Tell me, how many people work there in the office?'

'It's just me and two others,' the woman answered. By now it was obvious that what little interest she had had in talking to Norm was gone.

'No, I mean at the Anoisia office.'

'Sir, I told you there are no employees in that office! It's just a brass plate, that's all.'

'What? A 'brass plate'? What's that?'

'I'm sorry sir,' the woman said, finally a note of kindness in her voice. 'I assumed that you knew a little more about the business here. A brass plate is what we call about ninety percent of the registered businesses here in the Bahamas. They are companies officially domiciled here but they normally don't have any staff. Sometimes there's one person signing forms and answering the phone – if it ever rings. They don't really do anything.'

Norm quickly scanned the list of worldwide Anoisia offices in the annual report and put his finger on the other two offices in The Bahamas. 'What about Anoisia Bahamas North America, or Anoisia Europe Bahamas,' he asked. 'Do you happen to know anything about either of those offices?'

'Yes, same thing. We handle them, too.'

'So,' Norm began without being sure of what it was that he wanted to ask. 'Well, okay, thanks very much.'

Norm hung up the phone and stared blankly into his computer screen as he watched his screensaver, the Anoisia logo, fading in and out of view in various locations like a phantom that had possessed his machine. As it morphed in and out of existence Norm thought of a fellow named Ben he had met through an article he had written for the company newspaper who worked in the accounting department in Anoisia Paris and picked up the phone again. Ben was a real talker. When Norm had spoken to him before to ask about recent changes in the international accounting standards that Anoisia in Europe adhered to, he found himself stuck on the phone for over an hour as Ben went through every possible interpretation of the changes and how they might affect the company. Norm thought he might be the perfect person to help him figure out what was puzzling him.

He was right.

When he asked him if he knew anything about the offices in the Bahamas Ben laughed. 'A little hiding place, if you ask me,' he had said. 'Just a black hole for debt.' Minutes later, Norm was thanking him and walking out the door to the elevator heading for the eighth floor, where the accounting department was.

Norm sat in the corner of the café nestled into the hangar-like vastness of the first floor of the Anoisia building and stared at his empty plate as he realized that he had run out of ideas for how to bring up the subject with Shannon, so he just looked up at her and stared as she sat across from him, smiling as she licked the tip of her finger and pressed it to the crumbs on her plate that were the only thing left of her turkey and avocado sandwich.

'What?' she asked him, pushing her plate forward and sucking gently on her finger before taking Norm's hand.

'Anoisia Bahamas,' Norm said, watching for the reaction that was to come swiftly. Shannon let Norm's hand go. Her eyes went wide. Her expression seemed merely one of surprise and curiosity at first. Then Norm saw that it had been a smokescreen as her grin slipped and she began to look very pale.

'Oh Norm!' she cried, her hands holding her head as she sat forward and rested her elbows on the table. 'Of course I knew something was wrong when I saw our results. I knew we'd had a bad year, but I didn't know enough beforehand to do anything. I'm just a gopher here.' She was close to tears. 'I feel like I'm going to be sick,' she said, placing a hand over her stomach.

'Here, have a sip.' Norm handed her his bottle of mineral water. 'It's cold. It'll make you feel better.'

Shannon had a sip of the water, and then another before slowly returning it to the table, questioning Norm with her eyes.

'I read through the annual report today,' Norm explained. 'I read all the notes. And I wondered about these new Bahamas companies, so I phoned them up. Their phone numbers are right there in the back of the report for anyone to see.' He crossed his arms over his chest and then uncrossed them, taking Shannon's hand and giving it a squeeze. 'Just phoned them up,' he repeated. Norm saw that Shannon's eyes were growing moist.

His mind was made up. His little sister Emily would be pleased when he told her what he planned to do.

'We've got our first big post-results meeting tomorrow, as you know,' he said, his eyes sparkling. 'What do you think? You think Mr. Russell still likes it when we 'tell it like it is'?'

Shannon's eyes grew wide as she brought her hand to her mouth.

'Nonsense!' she cried.

The word rang in Norm's ears and danced around his brain for a moment as he finally remembered, and then realized why Anoisia seemed familiar, as if it meant something to him. Now, it did mean something. Norm smiled inwardly: the Greek and Latin classes weren't a waste after all.

"Nonsense'?' he asked. 'No, Anoisia!' He smiled at her, but Shannon failed to find the humor in his remark. 'Come on, Shannon, they're going to find it anyway. The analysts. It won't take long, so what difference does it make? I've enjoyed working here. But it won't be so bad. I'll find something else. Besides,' he said, feeling the warmth of Shannon's hand, 'I've got you, now.'

Anoisia: noun (Greek) *nonsense*

Lisa the Goat

I will never forget the first time I saw the old woman. She almost killed me. Not on purpose, but if it were to have happened, well. Dead is dead, isn't it? I have many faults, naturally, but by far the worst, in terms of the potential danger it causes to me, is that I have a habit of not paying attention to things like roads and cars. Roads and cars. Cars and roads. When you have one, sooner or later you have the other. They belong together. It's something worth remembering, but I seem to have a kind of mental block when it comes to that. All the other goats run when a car comes. But me, I seem to have a blind spot for them. I'll never be able to explain it.

It was the beginning of summer, the days were getting very long, the grass was good, flowers were still blooming, and the people were getting more excited because the tourists would start showing up soon and make everyone get busy. It was early morning. I had just been gazing out over the sea, as I like to do, and felt sleep coming on. And I do like to sleep. It's especially nice to nap just after getting my fill of grass and flowers, before the sun starts to really burn and it gets a bit too hot to sleep like that, out in the open. So I turned and headed away from the water, and suddenly I had an itch in my back. I looked down and the grass had turned to dirt, and there were little stones scattered here and there at my feet, so I lay down in that dirt and in those stones and rolled and wriggled until I felt the pleasure of the itch being put to rest by the earth beneath me. Ohhh, it felt so good. I lay there for a moment thinking about how nice it was to be able to scratch an itch, and then I closed my eyes and must have dozed off right there in the road.

I began dreaming almost right away. Of him.

He was someone I knew well, but only in dreams. Sometimes I knew him by sight, and other times I knew him simply because I could feel him. I could feel that it was him. The one I love. He was strong, and dark, and always smelled so wonderful. He wasn't like any of the rest. I loved him, but as I said, I only knew him in my dreams. He was real, but I had to enter my dreams to find him. And even then, I wasn't always able to find him. In fact, I was powerless in that regard. He either appeared, or he didn't. I loved him, but that kind of love is very painful. Because when I would awaken, he would be gone. I would be back in this world, alone. Or at least, without him. On my own, in a world where I had no love.

On this day, as I said, I began dreaming immediately, and out of nowhere, there he was. He came striding right up to me, his beard blowing in the wind, his eyes smiling, and in seconds my face was buried in his and I began to lose control. Don't ever let anyone tell you that love isn't anything special. It is. Even when we only know it in this way. In dreams. You see, I lived for this. I kept up the hope that I would meet him one day out by the sea. And I did look for him. Wandered much farther than I ought to have. But he remained a dream. Anyway, on that day, we were together, and I was swallowed by his warmth, my eyes closed against his dark hair, when all of a sudden he pulled his head back and said 'someone's coming!' And the shock of it woke me up. I sat up and the sun hit me squarely in the face and I tried to get my bearings, and then I was gripped by a feeling that something horrible was about to happen. Then I saw the car, bearing right down on me. There was a noise around me like a hundred thunderbolts firing all at once. I froze. Couldn't move a muscle. And in the instant that I realized that I was a goner, the car stopped and everything was quiet. The door opened and out she came, looking right at me. She squinted her eyes at me and then smiled. What a face she had. Like a statue.

She looked out over the sea and I stared at her profile. She was truly lovely. With milky skin, a proud nose, a thoughtful mouth, and large green eyes. She spoke to me then. Softly and without rushing, like the wind through the pine trees. 'Well, hello there darling,' she said to me. 'I thought I saw something warm and furry curled up on the road in front of me.' I must have given her an odd stare or something, because she stopped talking then and considered me for a moment and then frowned and bent forward. 'I guess you don't understand Russian, do you?' she asked me. She laughed and stood up straight. 'Well, I don't speak Greek – yet – but I promise you I plan to learn.' She tried to explain to me later what a taxi cab was but I never did understand why someone would pay to be carried around in one of those horrible machines.

As I was standing there in the road, still shaking like falling flower petals, she told the big machine to go away after dragging a big box behind her. Then it was just the two of us. She stood there smiling at me and told me her name was Anna.

She went up to the old house, moving silently, carefully. She left her big box on wheels standing on the grass in front of the house like a present that you just won't ever be able to hide. The house was, like houses are, made of stone, with walls as thick as my belly. It used to be painted white, like houses are, but the old house had lost its paint some time ago. It was very simple and built on a simple rectangular base, with a door in front right in the middle. It was split into two spaces lengthwise, with the whole front space being one, single, wide room, and the back space being a kitchen in one corner, and the bedroom was in the other corner. In between them was the place where people cleaned and washed themselves. And that was all there was. Anna stood looking at the door that stood slightly open and took out a piece of paper from her pocket, looked at it, and began calling out.

'Mr. Papi...Papi-DA-po-lis...?' She looked at me and shrugged. 'Can you read?' she asked me. I kicked a stone and then took a few steps closer to have a better look at her piece of paper. 'Lisa. That's what I'll call you. You will be my Lisa. Lisa the goat.' I nodded and then tried again to maneuver closer to the piece of paper she held, but she snatched it away from me. 'Oh, no you don't!' She patted me on the head the way some people do. 'Mr. Papi-DA-polis?' she cried out. She looked at me and held me in her gaze, and thought of something to say. I love it how she does that. 'You are so pretty. I just came down here from Switzerland to live. Have you ever been to Switzerland?' I told her that I hadn't. She looked out over the sea. 'Switzerland is that way,' she said, and held her arm out straight, and pointed with her finger. Something I always wished I could do. 'But I'm not Swiss. I'm Russian. I don't suppose you've ever been to Russia either. Switzerland's a bit more comfortable. Smaller too. Like Greece.' She looked at the sea again and then at our surroundings. She breathed in deeply. 'This is what I need. The sea, the salt.' She squatted down and reached out to touch me. 'My man will be coming, too,' she said. 'Soon.' She stood up and looked at the sea. 'That's what he told me. 'Soon.' '

'I have a man too,' I told her, but I wasn't sure how to explain to her that he lived in my dreams and that I had not yet found him here.

She pointed to a ship that was sailing off into the distance. She said nothing, then. Just looked. Just watched. Then, in a very soft voice, she said 'He will come on a ship like that one. He will come, right here.' She looked at me and smiled. She turned and looked at the house, then looked up the road from where she had come. 'I need to find this man!'

Then I realized who she was looking for. It was Papi. So I told her. 'Papi,' I cried. 'Papi. He's over here!' I ran off toward Papi's house, then stopped, looking over my shoulder. Anna just stared at me a second and then went around behind the old house. Behind the back of it. So I lay down and waited for her to finish her inspection of the old place. But almost as soon as I lay down I was restless so I got to my feet and ran across the road over to the edge to look at the sea again. The wind was kicking up and I closed my eyes and smelled the salty air. Then I went over to the spot in the road where I had been napping and stood there a minute. Then lay down again. Trying to feel him. But he wasn't there anymore. I closed my eyes, but... nothing. Then Anna appeared at the corner of the old house. She looked concerned. 'There's nobody here,' she said softly to no one.

I raised my head and looked in her direction. Then I was on my feet and ran over to her again. 'Papi! He's over here, come!' This time she followed me, leaving her gift standing in front of the old house Papi used to live in.

I raced up to the top of the grade and stopped. I was much faster than Anna. Of course, I'm faster than all the people. I don't even have to try. It's easy. I waited for her and watched as she smiled at me and walked straight towards me. It was then that I noticed that she had a very nice way of walking. She moved smoothly, like a cat. I knew then that Papi was going to like her a lot. He always did like women who moved like that. Papi, the man who owned three cats himself. So, of course. It was clear as day. Some people said that Papi liked all the ladies, but I knew that wasn't true. No one can like everyone. You can try, but it doesn't work. You can have a really nice heart, like Anna does, one that seems to ooze love for everything under the sun, but even then. Even then, we can't do that. Do you know why? It's because others think about us too. And they might like us, and they might not. For whatever reason. And if they don't like us, we usually know it. And it's that knowing, you see, that gets under our skin and starts to wiggle. We can never ignore that, because when we know something, we know it. That's that. There's nothing you can do about what you know and what you don't know. You can't choose to know something, for example. You can't just say what you know, or what you believe, just because you want to. It isn't something you do, it just happens.

I realized then that I had just been staring straight off into space. 'Come!' I shouted to Anna.

'I'm coming,' she told me. In a moment she stood by my side and could see right down the other side of the grade onto Papi's house.

'Oh!' Anna said. 'It's beautiful.' She was surprised because from down below, of course, you can't see the house. Papi's old house sits at the end of the road, or so it would seem. It's easy to think that the world just ends right there, but of course, it doesn't. 'Maybe that's where he lives.'

We stood there, the two of us, looking down at Papi's house. I will never forget that moment either. She reached down and touched me and before I could stop myself I took the tip of her finger between my lips and gave it a kiss. I thought she would cry out and pull her hand away, like so many do. But she didn't seem to mind. She liked it, in fact. I knew it because she looked at me and I saw the corner of her mouth curl. She was like that. So calm. Not like the others. Right then I knew that we would be friends, she and I. I bumped her with my butt and set off down the hill shouting for Papi, but as I went down the hill I happened to glance left towards the beach and noticed that his boat was gone. Of course! He was out fishing, pulling in his nets with Stefanos. He would be out until the sun went lower. I stopped and turned to tell Anna, but she just continued on down the road, heading straight for the house. I knew what would happen. She would find the house empty and start to worry. I ran on ahead and pushed on the door with my nose. As usual, Papi hadn't closed it all the way. I walked in and let the door open all the way, and turned to Anna. 'Papi's out fishing,' I told her. 'You should come inside and wait. He'll be home eventually.'

Anna came over to the door. 'Mr. Papidopulos,' she called.

'He isn't here,' I told her again. I backed up a couple of steps into the house. Anna looked at me and beckoned with her arms.

'Hey,' she said, 'come on out. You probably shouldn't be inside the house.' Then she stepped inside. She squat down and held her hand out. 'Come,' she told me, but I wanted her to stay so I wasn't moving an inch. Then she turned her head and glanced around the house.

The new house was the same as the old house, only bigger. Like the old house, it only had four rooms: a big one in front, as wide as the house. Then a kitchen in the corner, the bedroom in the other corner, and the washing room in the middle. But as I said, it was bigger. I could run my fastest in the big room if I ran from one end to the other. 'Oh my,' she said. I thought she was impressed by how beautiful the house was at first, but then I realized she must have been thinking something else. Maybe she was impressed by its size, I thought. I ran to the other end of the room and then back all the way across to the other side, as fast as I could. 'Hey, hey!' she cried, then she put her hands to her mouth and closed her eyes. She breathed in deeply and smiled at me, holding her breath. 'A goat is running around in the living room,' she said, and started to laugh. She laughed until she cried.

I looked but didn't see another goat. 'You mean me?' I asked her. She was still laughing but she was trying to stop, waving her hand in front of her face. Then she held her hand over her eyes. 'Well, he obviously isn't here. And he obviously hasn't had time to clean recently so until he comes back I'll just tidy up a bit, what do you think?'

I wasn't sure it was necessary and I told her so but she wasn't about to change her mind. She stood with her hands on her hips and nodded to herself. 'Okay, let's get started.' She went to the kitchen and started moving things around and seemed to be happy so I went outside to wait for Papi to come back. I went over to the pier where Papi tied up his boat and walked out to the very end of it. I wanted to be there when he returned so I could tell him about our guest. It was my favorite time of day. The sun was getting low in the sky and everything shone in a golden brilliance. I thought of him then. My man. I couldn't help it. When something is beautiful, I often think of him. It just happens. I looked out to sea and watched the waves rolling and dancing. They were shining like thousands of little diamonds. I found a good spot and curled up right there and lay myself down. Might as well get some sleep, I thought. Maybe I will even meet my man again. I closed my eyes and felt the heat of the day warm me up. The woman was cleaning, and I was helping too. Everything was good. I think I must have fallen asleep right away. To the sound of waves.

I didn't see my man. I stood in the middle of a lush green field and was torn between lowering my head to eat the grass, and looking for my man. I couldn't see him anywhere. But after a minute or two, I could feel him. I was standing under a bright sun. The wind blew and birds flew above me and called to me. And then I could feel him. Suddenly there was a warmth that seemed to enter my body from everywhere, and I smiled and turned. Where are you, I wanted to call out. Where are you, my love? But there was no one. Then the intensity of the feeling increased. It became centered on my ribcage. I looked to where it came from and the sky grew dark.

'Hello, my girl.'

I opened my eyes and found Anna, at my side, seated on the pier next to me, her bare feet dangling in the water. She sat there with her hand on my ribs, petting my fur. 'You're not my man,' I found myself saying before I knew it. Anna looked at me and smiled. She must have thought I was a bit dumb. Or maybe she knew that I had simply been confused, having just moments before been far away in my sleep. Where I had gone, of course, I couldn't have known. One doesn't know those things about one's dreams. One can see that as a pity. Or, as I do, one can see it as a source of wonder and mystery in one's life. Something to make it a bit more special. That's the way I had always felt. Life was a mystery, and everything in it is a mystery too.

Anna was a mystery. She had such a lovely face. A wise face. There was a wisdom in her eyes and in her expression that was quite rare. Or at least, it was rare to see such wisdom on someone with whom one was so little acquainted. I figured that because I knew so little about her and had only just met her, my impression of her must be right. When someone can make such an impression in such a short period of time, well, what else could it be? As I lay there looking at her, with her looking at me, I wondered then what she might be thinking. Was she also thinking that I was wise? 'What are you thinking?' I asked her.

'You are so pretty,' she said.

'You think so?'

'So pretty.'

Suddenly I had the feeling I was being perhaps a bit rude, just lying there. As I said, I didn't know her well. So I got up and turned a circle and then settled down bedside her. 'Thank you,' I told her. 'You're pretty too. But I'm sure you know that.' She looked out to sea then and closed her eyes, breathing in deeply. I joined her in considering the waves. We sat in our cove. The cove where Papi lived. One could see quite far down the coast to the left from where we were, but on our right, the rocks extended out into the sea and then disappeared around the corner. And around the corner, the coast ran a jagged line, forming many other coves just like this one. Some bigger, others smaller. But all of them the same, really. Papi lived, then, at the beginning – or the end, depending on how you looked at it – of this line of coves. On the other side, to our left, the coast ran fairly smoothly all the way to the village, then it cut back a bit, continuing in a more or less straight line, and then broke up into many coves, just like the ones that sat on the right of us. I knew that, not because I had wandered so far from home, but because sometimes Papi took me with him on his fishing boat and when he went fishing his favorite spot was off in that direction, so for a little while we headed along the coast there, until it fell away from us and we continued on straight, until we arrived at his spot. His favorite spot to fish.

I was sure that it was from this direction that he would come tonight, when he came home.

'It's lovely here,' she said. She looked back at the house, and then again at the sea. 'Where is that Mr. Papidopulos?'

She asked the question without any real interest, as one does when one is just talking to say something. I think she felt lonely. I also looked out to sea again. I got up and walked to the very end of the pier. I jumped up and down. Once. Twice. Trying to force something to happen. Then I had another idea and hurried off the pier and ran along the little beach and then up onto the rocks that stretched out into the water, and stopped when I was on the top. From there I could see much farther out, like a bird. Hovering. 'He's not here yet,' I called to Anna, who sat looking at Papi's house now. Then I looked back out to sea, and there he was. I could see his boat, the *Helios*, doing its best to get back home, up and down, over the waves. When I looked at Anna to tell her that he was coming, she was already standing on the pier looking in his direction. We must have found him at the same time. She stood with her hand over her brow, blocking the sun from her eyes. It was clear that she had seen him. But I couldn't help it, I cried out anyway. 'He's coming!' I ran down the rocks and back to the pier. Anna was nervous.

'Do you think he'll mind that I tidied up a bit for him?' she asked me without taking her eyes off the boat.

'He might,' I told her. I felt bad as soon as I said it, but I guess I thought we knew each other well enough by then that

I should be honest with her. She looked at me but merely smiled and then reached down to stroke my neck.

The *Helios* was one of the nicer fishing boats around. She was painted white and blue, and was always clean. Papi was very particular about his boat. He spent a lot of time taking care of her. Cleaning her, painting, repairing, hitting her with his hammer. Sometimes he even read books to her. He would climb in and sit on the bow – he normally brought a big pillow then – and he'd read to her, quietly. One thing was sure, he loved his boat. Now as they came in, Papi stood with one hand on the door frame of the cabin, and the other hand on the steering wheel. Stefanos was at the bow, ready to jump onto the pier. Papi and Stefanos were talking and laughing as *Helios* approached the pier. They must have had a good time with the fish. I looked at Anna. She smiled and waited for them as they came closer and closer. She reached up and moved her hair with her hand.

'Hello,' she called out. Just then, Stefanos jumped from the bow of the boat onto the pier, with one end of a rope in his hand, and then turned around again, pushing the boat with his foot so that it would not strike the pier. He took the rope and quickly tied it to the pier, then stood up and looked at Anna. 'Hello,' she said to him.

Stefanos smiled at her. Stefanos was tall and wiry, but very strong. Fisherman strong. He was twenty-eight years old and had hair that was almost straight. On the whole island, his dark, charcoal colored hair was the straightest. He had no curls, but merely some gentle waves, like the sea early in the morning. In fact, his entire face shared this same feature. His eyes, mouth and nose all pitched in to lend his face a soft, wavy look. It was for that reason that many women on the island considered him to be very special.

'Hello,' he said. I was amused because I knew that Anna didn't know which one Papi was. But I did. As it occurred to me, I looked at Papi and couldn't believe what I saw. He stood at the cabin looking at Anna with his hand on the wheel and had that look on his face like he had when he drank a lot of ouzo. Had he been drinking on the boat? Was that why he liked going out on the boat so much? Papi loves ouzo so much that sometimes he falls down when he can't have any more. I don't like ouzo. I tried drinking some of it once when

Papi had a bottle of it and it fell over. It spilled out and I was so thirsty that I licked at the water that was coming out of the bottle but it was not water and made a fire in my mouth and I thought I would die. I ran to my big bucket then and put my mouth in it and then it felt much better. My bucket was filled with water, which looks just like ouzo. I don't even know what ouzo is but I know that I have to stay far away from it. But it doesn't burn Papi like it does me. Or maybe it only burns inside his head and not in his mouth, because he never runs away from it. Anyway, Papi stood there on *Helios* and the way he looked, well I couldn't see any bottles of ouzo nearby but I know that look. I had to warn Anna, because when Papi has been drinking ouzo he can be a little unpredictable. 'Anna, watch out!' I said. 'Papi's got ouzo inside him.'

But Anna didn't hear me. 'Hello, are you Mr. Papidopulos?' she asked Stefanos. Stefanos looked over at Papi and Papi smiled at him. Then he looked at me and smiled. And like magic, he no longer had that ouzo look on his face. Papi stepped away from the cabin then and went towards the back of the boat, picked up a line that was coiled there, and stepped off lightly onto the pier. He pulled the line, snugging the boat against the pier, and then tied it off. He turned then and approached us. He stopped in front of Anna and raised his hand.

'Are you Anna?' Papi asked.

Anna took his hand and, for some reason, looked at me a second before answering. 'Yes.'

'I'm Demitrius Papidopulos.' Papi then raised his arm and swept it over the beach and the house. 'Welcome,' he said. Anna nodded and thanked him. And then she looked at Stefanos, and then at the boat. 'Oh, this is Stefanos, my good friend. He's the muscle for an old fisherman.' He said, smiling at Stefanos and then at Anna. 'My English is rusty! You'll help me get my English back,' he told her.

Anna did not know what to say. 'Your English is very good. But I'm hoping to learn some Greek, too. So maybe we can make a trade?'

Papi laughed out loud. 'Yes, why not?'

Anna nodded to him and then looked behind him at the boat. 'Did you catch anything, Mr. Papidopulos?'

'Oh, please, call me Demitri,' Papi said, and then looked at the *Helios* and beamed at her. 'Yes, and we had a fine day. Really perfect.'

'Oh, how lovely,' Anna said. Papi tilted his head at her comment and then felt embarrassed that she might have noticed his reaction. He nodded.

'Yes, lovely,' he said. 'In fact, we must unload the fish now.' He looked at Stefanos and nodded, turning to the boat. Then he turned again. His eyebrows sat high on his forehead. 'Oh, would you like to watch? The fish are beautiful!'

Anna smiled at him. 'Yes, of course.'

'Do you need anything? Are you thirsty?' Papi suddenly came back to Anna. He was embarrassed that he had forgotten to ask after her. 'Was your trip alright?'

'Yes, my trip was easy, and no, I'm fine. Please, do your work. I don't want to interrupt your work, really.'

Anna was very polite. Papi nodded and showed her how big with his hands. 'You like to eat a big fish tonight? We caught a few nice grouper fish, really big ones!'

'Yes, that would be wonderful.'

Papi smiled and nodded. 'Good. I will bake it *plaki*-style for you. You like onions?'

'Yes, I love food and I'm not picky,' Anna told him. Papi turned to step back onto the boat but then stopped and looked at Anna. She came over to me and knelt by my side and put her arm around my neck. Papi had that ouzo look on his face again but now I knew he had none of it. He put his hands together the way he does sometimes when he talks to the sky, but he never took his eyes off of Anna.

'You like her? She's a nice goat, isn't she?'

Anna nodded and massaged my neck with her fingers. A warm prickly feeling ran through my body and I could hardly move, but I wanted to. I was so happy I wanted to run and jump! But I just stood there. And then I thought: maybe it wasn't ouzo at all.

'I called her Lisa,' Anna said.

'Lisa? Really? You gave her a name?' Papi laughed. Then I noticed Stefanos looking at Papi in a very strange way and Papi must have felt that because he looked at Stefanos – it was like he had forgotten all about him – and he made his face very flat. 'Well, let's get this boat unloaded!' he said, and he stomped down the pier and climbed into the *Helios*. 'Stefanos, I hand the tubs to you. Come on over.'

The fish were kept in large plastic tubs. Papi picked them up and set them on the edge of the boat, where Stefanos took them and set them down on the pier with a big 'crack'. There were four tubs and they looked very heavy the way Papi and Stefanos were moving them. When all four tubs were on the pier, Papi stopped and wiped his forehead with his handkerchief. 'Okay, take out two big groupers and put them in my cold box and bring the rest into the market. And when you're there, tell Cosima my Russian lady is here and that she should have dinner with us tonight. Tell Despina too.' Stefano nodded his head. Papi looked at Anna and became very quiet. Then his eyes jumped and he started toward her. 'So, let's get you to your new place, okay? You follow me,' he said. He took Anna by the hand and led her for a few steps along the pier and then let go of her hand and started searching through his pockets for his handkerchief. I ran ahead of them and stopped at the front of the pier. Papi patted my head when he walked by. That was what I was waiting for.

* * *

Demitrius Papidopulos had not been at all annoyed with Anna for having tidied his house a bit while she waited for him to arrive. In fact, he was grateful. But he was unprepared for her suggestion that he allow her to put "a bit of make-up" on the house in preparation for the dinner party. 'I will need some string, and some scissors, and some wire,' Anna told Demitrius.

These were things that any fisherman had in abundance, so it was not a problem in the least for Demitrius to get them for Anna. Supplied with the string, scissors and wire, Anna set to work while Demitrius worked on his boat. Anna found sea shells, odd pieces of sunburned wood, bits of colorful paper that she folded magically into animal forms, chunks of smooth, colored glass out behind the house that had been worn smooth by the water and sand over years, and she tied them to the string and hung them from the ceiling of the living room, across from one side to the other and back again.

When she was finished she went out with her notebook and sat on the pier and watched the sea.

As he worked, Demitrius stole glances at the woman who came from far away with eyes that seemed to him to hold stories of love and squalor alien to him and yet made, somehow, just for him to hear. He watched her, now and again, as she sat on the edge of the pier, one moment gazing out over the waves, the other hard at work on her writing. Somehow it was a kind of comfort to him, that the both of them should be at work on what they loved so much. His work came to him so easily, he thought to himself. For when the goal was so clear – to catch fish – there could be no confusion over what needed to be done. A series of goals dictated every action. Getting a fish on a line meant getting a line prepared and in the water. Or if one were using nets, then getting the nets prepared and in the water. Going out on the boat required preparation, too. The boat needed fuel. The engine needed regular servicing. Fishing supplies had to be cared for. One had to have something to eat and drink on board. The boat had to be cleaned after the day's effort. All of these things were obvious if one simply considered the goal. But what of the woman whose goal was to write? Was it similarly clear what had to be done? Would a series of goals allow work to be carried out as clearly and without confusion as his own?

Demitrius finished tightening the spark plug that he had just cleaned and gapped and closed the engine bay, locking the lid and then resting a moment on it. He took a cloth from his pocket and wiped the spark plug wrench clean as he checked Anna's progress once more. She looked out over the water, a neutral expression on her face. Then she looked at him and he saw a flicker of sadness jump from her eyes before being pushed aside by a warm smile that landed directly on the center of his being. His ears grew warm and he found himself smiling back at her, but aware that her work was not so simple as his own.

When he had finished the last of his tasks, cleaning the windows on the *Helios*, Demitrius stepped off of the boat and onto the pier and took a seat beside Anna at the pier's end, letting his feet hang over the edge, his shoes just inches above the water that was constantly in motion as it settled itself over and over again. Anna took a long look at Demitrius as he sat down next to her. He had managed, she thought then, to keep himself in a very good condition for a man who apparently spent a considerable amount of time on a boat in the ocean doing hard work. His hands were what she noticed first. Although strong and round and powerful, they were not dry, cracked and beaten as she realized then she was expecting them to be. Neither was his face. Although tanned and rugged, his face did not look as though it had merely survived the sun, wind and water. She looked then at the fisherman's clothes. There, she found no torn bits of cloth, no holes in the fabric, no dried and smelly remains of fish on his canvas pants and long-sleeved cotton shirt. She noticed then Demitrius was watching her observing him. He smiled at her.

'Your hands,' she started. 'They look...' and then she stumbled, unsure of how to describe them without insulting this man whom she felt comfortable with but whom she reminded herself she hardly knew, and would surely depend on in the coming weeks and months.

'Yes?' Demitrius prompted her, his smile deepening.

Suddenly Anna no longer felt comfortable with her intended comments. She shook her head. 'Nothing,' she said. 'I just would have expected them to be quite awful, I suppose.'

Later she helped Demitrius in the kitchen. After helping clean the fish and cut some vegetables, she stood back and watched him take it from there. The dishes Demitrius prepared were simple. Not in need of so many hands. But she observed him, and served him ouzo and Mantinian white wine, which she gladly drank right along with him. He was full of life and laughed a lot, which suited Anna just fine.

He told her the story of his life. Of how he came with his parents from Athens, 'that big, dirty city,' as a boy, to the island that his parents had been born and raised on before setting off in search of bigger things. An education in the small local school, an apprenticeship as a carpenter that evolved into following his teacher on his real love of fishing, which then became his own passion.

'And a woman?' Anna asked him. 'When does she come into the picture?'

But Demitrius merely smiled and shrugged at her question. 'Well,' he announced, raising his finger, 'I have had many loves, I will say that.' He looked Anna in the eye and then his gaze shifted into the room behind her. 'Okay, so there was one woman who was special. This was many years ago,' he offered, rubbing his wet hands on the towel that hung at his waist. He took another sip of ouzo and then poured and offered Anna some more as well. 'She was Grace. Or, Grace was her name. She was American.'

'A tourist?' Anna asked him.

He nodded. 'She saw me cleaning my boat at the docks in the village and became curious. We started talking and she asked if I would take her fishing. Her and her friend Marlene. Two crazy girls,' he said, memories shining in his eyes from the day they spent on the boat. 'And she was special. So I went to visit her in San Francisco and lived there for almost a year. That's where I really learned to speak English.'

Anna nodded and smiled at the rugged, attractive man who stood before him exuding a wistful joy at the memories of love he held within him, with no sign of bitterness, pain or regret. She wondered at the possibility of being a deep and sensitive person, such as Demitrius clearly was, and to have escaped from the love of his life without the pain that would certainly be the silver bullet that would make talking of such things impossible for her. She turned the wine glass in her hand by the stem back and forth and then glanced out through the living room window and was surprised to see the ocean. 'Yes, I am on an island,' she reminded herself, unable to stop the smile on her lips from spreading across her face.

'Well,' she started, coming back to things. 'That must have been quite a change for you, San Francisco.'

Demitrius smiled and shrugged. 'Yes, it was. But luckily for me, I still had the sea. And what a sea it is!' he exclaimed, his hands moving in a wide arc and spilling the rest of his ouzo onto the floor. Anna noted with amusement how his reaction to this was to do nothing more than glance at the floor and then set his glass on the counter next to the sink and carry on with his story. 'The Pacific ocean is a real wilderness. The waves, the winds, the fish.' He looked out the window and pointed at the Mediterranean with his chin. 'This is just a pond,' he said. 'I tell you, once I was out fishing – that's what I did while I was there after about a month, you see. I got a job as a fisherman, taking people out for sport fishing. I worked for a man - Gus was his name - on a fifteen meter boat called *Lucky Lady*,' he said, pausing to smile at the recollection. He put his hands on his hips and shook his head. 'We had some times, Gus and I... but well, this one time, it was a group of bankers and they wanted to go fishing. So we went out, and on this day the *Lady* was not very lucky. And these boys started getting a little annoyed and then BANG! Just like that, one of them gets a hit on his line and starts shouting and pulling and I could see it was something big and so we pulled in our lines and the fight was on. Well, it turns out this guy had a shark on the line. And not just any shark, no. This was a Great White shark, you see? The JAWS shark, from the movies.'

'Oh my,' Anna said, her expression revealing her question as to in what gruesome direction the story might turn.

'No, no, it's nothing bad,' Demitrius reassured her. 'So he had to fight with this shark for about an hour and he was getting really tired, but the shark was getting tired too. And so the shark, he swims up to the back of the boat and he puts his head out of the water and this young banker saw the shark with his big teeth and you know what he did? He let go of his fishing pole! No, he really actually threw it away from himself, like it was on fire! He was so frightened when he saw that shark! And so his pole goes flying into the water and we all turned to look at him, you know, we were all so surprised. And then he said 'Oh, I'm going to be sick!' he says. Hah! Can you believe it?' Demitrius rolled his eyes and waved his hands before turning to find the wine and topping up their glasses. Feeling that the wine was no longer suitably cold he put it in his small refrigerator and then picked up his glass and held it out to Anna.

'*Yiamas*,' he said.

'*Yiamas*,' Anna replied.

'To good times, and new friends,' Demitrius said.

Anna nodded and felt herself blushing.

'Oh, what am I?' she asked herself aloud. 'Am I a teenager?' she put a hand to her cheek and laughed, shaking her head and waving for him to continue when Demitrius raised his eyebrows in question at her comment. 'So then what happened?' Anna asked him. Demitrius looked at his watch and then motioned for Anna to join him at the table in the living room. The two of them stepped out of the kitchen and into the living room where Demitrius pulled a chair out from the table for Anna to sit. Demitrius couldn't help asking. The words just slipped out.

'Tell me,' he asked, 'What about your husband?'

Anna saw the change in Demitrius's expression just then and looked away, not wishing to intrude. She knew it. Or rather, she had known, or had felt something from him. But now, she really knew. She wondered if he himself knew. She felt the familiar wave of pleasure at being desired. At her age, this was an especially nice feeling to have. She hesitated, knowing that this innocent pleasure could not continue for either one of them. Not now. She shot Demitrius a look and wondered if he understood it: Why did you have to ask me this? It was a clear invitation, but one that he did not pick up.

'What can I tell you about him? His name is John. He is English, but he was raised here and there and everywhere. You can't pick out his accent,' she said, her eyes focused on the wine in her glass that shot out bolts of light reflected from the lamp overhead. Just then she had a picture of him in her mind and felt a warmth spread through her body.

Demitrius watched this fine woman, who was now temporarily unable to speak. 'You can't?' he asked.

Anna raised her glass off of the table, but only just, and then set it down again. 'No. He doesn't really have one, you see. But it's a nice accent. Soothing. Soft.'

Demitrius shifted his weight in his chair and looked out over the table, but everything was set and prepared and there was nothing else left to do. 'And what does he do?'

'Well, before he retired he was a philosophy professor,' Anna told him.

Demitrius pursed his lips, forced something resembling a smile and nodded. He had never understood the philosophers. Or so he thought. Without knowing it, he had understood very well the impulse driving them, but their expression of this impulse escaped him. 'So, I suppose he will be able to speak to me in my own language?'

Anna nodded. 'Yes, he can speak some Greek, but of course he reads it much better than he can speak it.'

'And now?' Demitrius asked. 'What does he do?'

'Now he builds furniture,' Anna told him. This answer inspired respect, and jealousy, in the fisherman, who nodded and raised his eyebrows. He glanced at the small wooden table near the light switch at the door to his home, the one with the wooden bowl on it that he emptied his pockets into when he came home. The one with the torn off piece of a paper beer coaster from the bar in town, stuck under the third leg to keep the table steady. He pursed his lips and laced his fingers together. 'That's a nice hobby.'

Anna held a tuft of her hair between her fingers, and then gathered her hair together behind her head and tied it into a loose knot as she spoke. 'Yes, he loves building things. He had some of his pieces in a couple of shops in the city.'

'"Pieces?",' Demitrius asked. He knew what the English word meant but thought that it was something that would be used for artworks rather than for furniture.

'Yes. He builds things for friends from time to time but it's also nice for him to build and sell pieces. He has sold many things. Mainly tables, chairs and desks. He especially likes building desks. You know, the kind with lots of little drawers and places to hide things.'

Demitrius wanted to change the subject but now found himself too interested. 'And how did you meet?'

Anna closed her eyes and held the images in her mind for a moment before answering. 'We met in a park.'

'A park?'

'Yes. Near my apartment in the heart of the city. There is a park. It's built on a hill next to a river and so it rises to a kind of a peak, or a *Gipfel*, as the locals say. I often went there, living so near to it. One day, in summer, I went for a stroll and found myself standing at the top, surrounded by lush green trees, flowers and plants. It was a brilliant sky, on that day. Large, flat-bottomed fluffy clouds were sliding overhead with a lustrous blue background. And I noticed a man sitting on a bench nearby and went over to share it with him. I will never forget it. I was happy. Somehow thrilled, even, I remember, as I sat there. It was such a beautiful day. And I glanced over at the man and was surprised at what I saw. He had such a sad look on his face. Such a handsome face. A handsome man. But so sad. I was struck with sympathy for him and found myself, well, I stood and found myself moving nearer to him and sitting next to him. As I did, he looked up at me. I don't think he had really noticed me until then. And when he saw me, his sadness suddenly took on an embarrassed turn and...he smiled.'

Demitrius was listening intently, his breathing quickened by the tale Anna told. 'He smiled,' he repeated.

Anna looked at him and continued. 'Yes. He did. 'You have such sad eyes,' I told him. Ordinarily I would not have spoken to a stranger in such a way as this. In such an intimate way. But there was something about him that immediately struck me, and that made talking to him like this seem like a completely natural thing. Because I felt a connection to him, you see, a connection that I didn't understand but that I didn't need to understand either.'

'Yes,' Demitrius offered.

'Understanding is sometimes overrated, I'm afraid. Or at least I think so. Don't you?' Anna asked him. But Demitrius simply shrugged. Perhaps he didn't completely understand.

'Why was he so sad?' Demitrius asked.

Anna merely smiled and shook her head at his question as the memory faded. 'Perhaps you can ask him when he comes,' she said.

Demitrius accepted this answer with a nod and then looked toward the kitchen. 'Excuse me,' he said, as he rose and told himself that he was just a fisherman. He went into the kitchen and placed his hands on either side of the sink and stared out of the window into the fir trees behind the house. He looked down at his hands and touched the spots on the backs of them that he was still getting used to. So many years without them. They were still unwelcome. Still a mystery. The light in the trees was golden. Demitrius opened the window to listen to the sound of the golden light playing in the trees. As he strained to hear, he turned to see Anna standing behind him in the doorway, leaning faintly against the peeling white paint he had told himself last year he would touch up. She had her arms crossed over her chest, her head tilted, with a smile on her face that assured him he need not worry.

'The light is wonderful,' he told her, turning to face the trees for a moment. 'I came to get the ouzo,' he said, and fetched the bottle, then raised it toward the doorway, indicating that they would return to the table. 'Come,' he said. 'Our guests will arrive soon.'

They could both hear the crunching of footsteps and so looked toward the door which stood open. Stefano came in first carrying a large bag filled with wine and traditional desserts that he handed to Demitrius, then immediately beamed at and then shook hands with Anna, before turning and observing the two women who had remained outside, unseen. Anna watched as Stefano looked at the women outside, a tender expression on his face as he observed them.

Although when she thought about it later she knew she could not remember having spent a single moment thinking about them, but as Anna waited for the women to enter the house, with the tips of her fingers resting on the corner of the dining table, she had an image in her mind of two women at least as old as herself, dressed in simple peasant clothes that would be suitable for life herding goats or picking olives or any other similar activity that must have been the focus of this island life. She was surprised, and delighted, to see what did walk in the door after Stefano. Despina grew up on the island and worked in a bank in the town. She was tall, dark and lovely in her black party dress and spike heels and instantly reminded Anna of Maria Callas. Cosima entered after Despina and the two of them immediately looked up and marvelled at the decorations that hung from the ceiling. 'That is Anna's work,' Demitrius proudly offered, holding his arm out and indicating his new guest. The two women turned and nodded at Anna. Having moved to the island from Athens a few years ago, Cosima was the most popular hairdresser in town. She was very tanned, blond and pretty and, like Despina, wore a short party dress. Suddenly Anna knew why Stefano had had to wait for the women to enter the house. They must have walked the unpaved road to the house barefoot, putting their fine shoes on only upon arrival. Despina paused at Stefano's side and then took two steps forward, stopping directly in front of Anna. 'Hello,' she said, offering Anna her hand. 'I am Despina.' Cosima entered then as well and embraced Demitri as he came around from the other side of the table. He threw his arms around the woman and kissed her cheek, then moved on to Despina, allowing Cosima to approach Anna. '*Hari-ka Pu Sas Gno-ri-ssa*,' Cosima said, before switching to English. 'My name is Cosima.'

Anna took her hand and nodded. 'Hello Cosima, I'm Anna. I'm afraid I don't speak Greek.'

'Oh, of course,' Cosima replied. 'Nobody speaks Greek. Only us.' Anna tried guessing at their ages. Twenty-seven? Thirty-two? It wasn't easy. Neither of these women had spent their lives hauling fish nets or ploughing the sun-baked earth.

With his house filled with guests, Demitrius came alive, first showing everyone to the table and filling their wine glasses, then opening up his old hi-fi and placing a recording of Mikis Theodrakis on the platter.

'Oh, not old Mikis,' Stefano complained, making eye contact with Cosima and rolling his eyes good naturedly.

'Hey, my house, my music,' Demitrius told him. 'And besides, when it's finished you can choose something, how's that?'

'Yes old man,' Stefano told him, 'Don't get agitated now.'

Demitrius and Anna went into the kitchen and brought out the food, and in moments all were seated at the table with the smell of baked fish and onions filling the room.

After a basic introduction from Demitrius, Anna couldn't resist asking questions. 'So, how is it that you all know each other?' she asked to no one in particular. She was surprised to find herself seated amongst such young people in the modest home of a considerably older fisherman.

The three younger ones looked at each other, each of them wondering how to begin. After a moment's hesitation, Despina spoke up.

'Well,' she began, 'Stefanos and I have known each other since we were kids, you know. And I met Cosima in Athens in the university.'

'Yes,' Cosima added, 'I'm here because I came to visit Despina and to spend a summer here on the beach and then

I decided to stay. There weren't any good hairdressers here then,' she said, laughing at the memory of it. 'It was pretty easy to start my business here and to have a success from the start.'

'I see, well, that explains it.' Anna said, nodding. 'And how long have you been working with Demitrius, Stefano?'

All eyes went to Stefano, who had been looking into his wine glass absentmindedly, forcing him to sit up and take notice. Despina asked him something quickly in Greek, causing him to laugh and give an embarrassed nod of the head. 'Sorry,' he said, 'I not listening so much, you know...my English.'

'Oh, not at all,' Anna told him. 'No need to apologize.'

'This will be a good English lesson for you Stefano,' Demitrius told him, curling his meaty fingers into a fist and setting it in the middle of the table in front of Stefano.

'Yes,' Stefano agreed. 'So, I working with Demitrius long time.' He said simply, nodding to himself and considering the story finished.

After a moment of silence, the Greeks at the table produced a blizzard of conversation, then turned to Anna.

'They are asking what it is that you are writing,' Demitrius asked Anna as the eyes of all those present at the table fell upon her. Anna could not stop her mouth from falling open at the question.

'Please tell us,' Cosima asked her, with the attention and wonder of a child. Anna's eyes visited everyone then, one by one, as she wondered how she had failed to consider that at some point she might be asked this very question. For a brief moment she thought she had been saved when the notion to tell of one of her earlier works occurred to her. But as she opened her mouth to tell them the story of her first novel, *Love's Last Laugh*, she was struck by the realization that, of course, one of them could already know of that book. Who knew, perhaps all of them had read it? But no, it hadn't been translated into Greek – had it? She began running through an inventory of all of the languages *Love's Last Laugh* had been translated into when there came a pressure on her thigh that made her jump.

'Oh!' she cried, then looked down to see Lisa's chin on her leg, the goat's yellow eyes looking into her own.

'Come, you!' Demitrius snapped, reaching around the corner of the table toward Lisa.

'Oh no, Demitrius, it's okay,' Anna told him. 'Lisa's fine, aren't you my girl? No, she just startled me is all.'

'Sorry about that,' Demitrius said.

'It's okay,' Anna said, looking into Lisa's eyes and stroking her fur.

'Is it a secret, Anna?' Despina asked finally.

'What?' Anna asked.

'Your new book,' Despina reminded her.

'Well,' Anna began, answering all the genuine smiles directed at her with an impostor of her own, 'It's, you know, it's not exactly a secret...' Anna was flushed with embarrassment at her predicament and at her inability to carry on writing as she had for so many years. Somehow, the idea of telling them that she was simply suffering from writer's block and had not been able to get started on anything in over a year just didn't strike her as an option. No, in fact, it would have been a conversation killer. 'What am I writing? Oh, nothing. I have writer's block at the moment.' No, she would not tell them that she was a writer who could not write. She met the gazes of the others in an effort to somehow force her way into an answer.

'I would guess,' Demitrius began, 'that your publishers might not want you to talk about your work before it was published.' Anna searched Demitrius's face then, wondering if he was trying to save her from herself, wondering if he had figured out her problem.

'Yes, well, it's not as if...' Anna then checked herself. She had been about to say that it was not as if word of her new work could escape this tiny island and end up in some gossip column somewhere, but she realized how a comment like that might be perceived by the others. 'I mean, I can discuss my work with friends, of course.'

Lisa pushed her chin deeper into Anna's thigh, reminding her to continue to stroke and caress her fur. 'Yes Lisa,' Anna told her, looking down at her, grateful for this minor diversion from her ordeal. Lisa lifted her nose and looked directly into Anna's eyes. 'Yes, my lovely girl,' Anna told her, and in that instant, she found what she was looking for. 'I'm writing about Lisa. Lisa, the goat.'

Demitrius looked at Anna, and then at his goat. 'You're writing about my goat?' He held a guarded expression of surprise and amusement. Anna nodded.

'What does she say?' Stefano asked the others in Greek. Despina turned to him and told him that Anna was in fact writing about the goat. Stefano looked at Anna and nodded, slowly. He exchanged a few more words with Despina, who answered him and said the word 'goat' twice in English. Stefano repeated the word to her. Despina nodded.

'Good idea,' he told her. 'A goat story.'

'Are you really?' Demitrius asked Anna. 'And what *about* her?' he continued, without waiting for a reply.

'It's a story about a goat,' Anna announced with finality, hoping that this would end the discussion but realizing right away that it would do no such thing. She felt her face growing hot. What on earth was she thinking? What foolishness had she launched herself into?

'Please, tell us,' Cosima asked her again. A brief eruption of Greek flooded the table as the others reacted to the news and traded ideas and suspicions and jokes about what such a story might involve. Demitrius said nothing, however, and merely watched his friends with an amused look on his face, proud to know that Anna had decided to focus her efforts on something so close to home.

Anna stroked Lisa's fur again and looked into her eyes. What is your story, you pretty goat? Anna found it surprising how Lisa looked into her eyes, and how much warmth Anna seemed to find there, in the eyes of a goat. She smiled at Lisa and nodded as she spoke to her. 'Yes, my girl, you are lovely. You are indeed lovely.'

'Is she really a writer?' Stefano asked Demitrius, feeling slightly insulted at the sudden thought that he and the others were being fooled by this famous Ms. Nobody.

Demitrius's eyes flew open wide at the question. He knew Anna could not understand Greek but even so, the situation unnerved him. 'Yes she is, and we cannot talk about her in her presence! It's rude!'

'But why doesn't she tell us what the story is about?' Stefano replied.

'Dimitri,' Despina began, 'How do you know she's a writer, anyway? Have you ever read one of her books? I've never heard of her, to tell you the truth.'

'Me neither,' Stefano added.

'No, I haven't' Demitrius answered. 'But look, are you suggesting she's lying? And besides, I've seen her writing.'

'What, *here*?' Cosima asked.

'Yes here, out on the pier.'

'Writing what? Maybe she was just writing letters.'

'Letters?' Demitrius asked, showing his impatience with his hands. 'I don't think she would be writing letters in a notebook, or what do you think?' Demitrius sat up straight and lowered his voice and smiled. 'Now listen, not another word about my guest at this table.'

As the last words escaped Demitrius' lips, Anna cleared her throat and also sat up straight, raising her half full wine glass to her lips and draining it in one go. She placed her glass on the table and looked at Stefano, then at Cosima. 'Lisa is a goat living on a small Greek island, and she is in love,' she announced.

'What?' Stefano cried.

'She is in love.' Despina told him.

'Anna?'

'No, the goat. The goat is in love.' Despina then turned to Anna and gave her an encouraging look. 'Wonderful,' she said, nodding slowly.

Stefano leaned forward and his desperate eyes found Demitrius and the others. 'Who she is loving?' he asked Anna. 'The goat, who she is loving?'

'Well, who would you be in love with if you were a goat?' Anna asked him. Stefano did not seem to comprehend what she had said. 'She is in love with a goat,' she told him.

'Okay,' Stefano said to no one, in Greek. 'I guess this is something I do not need to read.'

Demitrius gave Stefano a hard look and poured Anna some more wine, then filled his own glass too before checking on the others. With the bottle empty, he rose and went to the kitchen to fetch another.

'Anna, do you often write about animals?' Despina asked her, trying to contain her sense of doubt at the idea.

Anna stared at Despina as the story started to simply fall into her lap. In order not to lose anything, she began telling the tale as it emerged from that place where unwritten stories come from, just as Demitrius returned to the table and sat down with the fourth bottle of wine.

Lisa, Anna told them, was in love with a goat in her dreams. But being a goat, she isn't aware of dreams as such, she simply knows that sometimes she is with her man and feels such a wonderful warmth, this feeling of love, that during that time she is happier than she has ever been. After this brief explanation, and as she started to feel the life and the story of Lisa the goat entering her heart, Anna placed her hands on her cheeks, overwhelmed at the notion that her writer's block seemed to be lifting.

'Anna,' Demitrius said, placing his hand upon her arm. 'Are you okay?' he asked, speaking softly.' Anna breathed deeply and nodded.

'Yes, yes, wonderful! I'm feeling just wonderful. Thank you.' She placed her hand upon his and found herself patting it gently.

'Okay,' Cosima said. 'So what's the problem?'

Anna turned to Cosima, who looked not at her but at Demitrius. 'I'm sorry?' Anna asked her.

'Well, with the goat. She's in love, so what's the problem?' Cosima asked again, the edge present in her voice a moment before now gone.

'Well, that's a good question,' Anna answered. 'The problem is that eventually, Lisa learns the difference between dreams and reality.'

With that, everyone at the table fell silent. Stefano, still trying to catch up, was intrigued. '*Ti ibbe*?' he asked anyone. 'What did she say?' As Cosima quietly explained to Stefano what Anna had said, Stefano nodded.

'Eh?' Demitrius asked him, 'not so stupid after all, huh?'

Stefano began to smile. Still nodding, he appeared to want to ask Anna something, but for whatever reason, was finding it difficult. Finally he leaned forward and laced his fingers together. 'Sorry Anna, my English...'

'Oh, nothing to fear,' Anna told him, placing her hand on his across the table. 'Please,' she invited him.

'So, you write this now? Here, on Naxos?'

'Yes!' Anna said with vigor.

At some point, the partygoers - every one of them it seemed, at the same time - realized that the music had stopped. Stefano sat up straight and looked at the quiet music box in the corner, such that the others took note and in a moment knew what had to happen next. 'The music,' Demitrius announced, getting up from his chair and rounding the table. He wondered as he went how many times he had made the trip to the music box that night. Was it five? Six times?

'Please, Demitrius,' Cosima called out to him, 'something modern this time?' Anna smiled and watched Demitrius to see how this criticism would be received. 'Otherwise I'll finally have to get up and dance to your folk music and throw some of these nice plates onto the floor.'

'Dancing!' Anna cried, 'Why, yes! That's a marvelous idea!' The words had hardly escaped her lips before she was up on her feet, hands clasped together and resting on her bosom. Demitrius was caught by surprise, half turned round as he stood at the music box with a look of disdain still on his face from Cosima's comment.

'Stefano, won't you show me a traditional Greek dance?' Anna asked, holding out her hand to the young man as he sat at the table grinning at Despina, whose hands rested on her hips, her chin raised to show the beauty of the curves of her neck to the young fisherman.

At this, Demitrius stood up straight, the wounded look now gone, replaced by one of determination. Instead of placing a new record on the turntable, he simply started the same record again. As the music began, he turned to his new guest. 'Anna, my dear, if you need a traditional Greek dancing teacher, Stefano is the wrong man to ask. Believe me, the kids these days know nothing about dancing.' He held out his hand toward Anna. 'Come, I will show you.'

Demitrius' accusation brought on stubborn cries of protest from the guests he had referred to as 'kids.' In seconds, the table was merely on display as the center of the living room saw Despina dancing with Stefano, and Cosima dancing all on her own, determined looks on their faces one moment, followed by embarrassed grins the next as they watched each other dancing like their parents had always done, but with a pride that surprised them all as it filled them and pushed them onwards. Demitrius held Anna's hand but was unable to begin his instruction, so surprised as he was at the joy shown by the others. Helpless, he looked at Anna, who nodded to him. 'You see? It seems they have learned something too,' she chided. She nodded one time, as if settling the matter. 'So,' she commanded, 'I will have my lesson now, yes?'

Demitrius adopted a similarly serious expression and nodded in reply. 'You will. Now, raise your arms, so, and watch me.'

And they danced, and they danced. Anna with Demitrius, then with Stefano, then with Despina while Cosima danced with Demitrius and Stefano filled their wine glasses. They danced on, and drank between songs, but always returned to the music as soon as the next number came, their enthusiasm growing with every turn. Demitrius became increasingly fond of Anna. Cosima fell more and more in love with Demitrius, and Stefano and Despina secretly wondered what it would be like to kiss the other. Anna became more and more determined to take up the story of Lisa the Goat the very next day. Lisa, pleased that everyone was enjoying themselves so much, lay curled up in the corner asleep, dreaming.

When the record was finished, five people returned to the table and emptied their water glasses. Stefano put the radio on and found his favorite station. Demitrius made no move to stop him. Instead, he went to the kitchen, bringing Anna with him. The two of them served the desserts Stefano brought. Cosima took care of the coffee. Demitrius opened another bottle of wine and poured himself a large glass after taking care of the others. Then he opened another bottle.

Demitrius had not felt inadequate being a fisherman in quite some time. But now, as he watched Anna listen to Cosima's stories of her trip to England from two years before, he recalled how, as they sat down to eat a few hours before, Anna had answered questions from the others about her husband. They had been simple questions, and had been answered simply. Anna had not dwelt on them, had not rambled on about her man, had not been bragging about him. But Demitrius found himself standing in comparison to him. What could he offer to a woman like Anna? Yes, he had had the feeling that she was showing - how should he think of it? *Some* kind of interest in him that was more than a casual interest. That was what it had been, he told himself. Whatever it was, it was enough. Enough for him to notice. And he knew he often didn't notice it when women took an interest in him. Anna's husband was a university teacher. Or had been one. Now, he made and sold 'pieces' of wooden furniture, or art, or whatever it was, while he, Demitrius, was just a fisherman.

Just a fisherman. He had always been proud to be a fisherman. Why? He knew very well why. He was his own man. He helped feed the community. He did honest work. And yes, it was romantic honest work. Something ancient. Yes, even poetic. It was certainly nothing to be ashamed about. No matter what Anna's husband was. And yet... Demitrius shook his head. What was he thinking, anyway? Anna was married. Her husband was coming soon to join her. What was he thinking?

Why was he still on his own, in fact, without any woman to come home to? After all these years. Demitrius stared into the candle flame on the table in front of him. He saw Anna rise and then sit next to him. She leaned close to him and the two of them watched as Stefano, Cosima and Despina discussed the approaching summer and how the tourists would make all of them busier.

'Demitrius, you know that Cosima is in love with you, don't you?' Anna asked him quietly, avoiding placing her hand on his arm so as not to draw too much of Cosima's attention.

Demitrius looked at Anna, surprised that she would come out with this so blatantly. 'Oh, I don't know,' he answered, also trying to keep his voice down. 'I suppose so. But she's so young. She's too young for me.' His eyes searched Anna's face, trying to read her thoughts. 'I need someone my own age,' he found himself saying to her.

Anna and Demitrius were interrupted by Cosima's laughter and instinctively shifted their gaze to her. She looked at them then, and they saw her smile slip. Anna saw the jealousy in Cosima's eyes. Demitrius did not. Cosima took a deep breath. At that moment, she felt unwell. Her eyes focused on her wine glass as she wondered for a moment how much she had drunk. A warm churning in her stomach forced her to her feet and propelled her towards the open front door. She stopped and leaned against the doorframe, putting her hand to her head as a breeze caught her hair. There, that was better. She opened her eyes, looking at the stony ground in front of the house, surprised to see so much light on the stones outside. She looked up and saw the blazing moon high above, filling the sky with an amazing light that danced on the waves. 'Oh my god,' she cried, in English. She turned to the others. 'Come, everyone, look outside! The moon!' She kicked off her shoes and padded out onto the soft silty ground, and the grass that grew in a multitude of struggling tufts. The cool breeze and the night air revived her, and moments later she wheeled round to welcome everyone to the world she had stumbled upon. 'Isn't it amazing?' she cried. The others were equally impressed as they stood outside, Stefano with his wine glass in hand and his arm casually around Despina's shoulders, Demitrius and Anna side by side just behind them.

'Dimi, take us out on the sea! Please!' Cosima cried, rushing over to Demitrius and taking him by the hand, pulling him towards his boat.

'Yes!' Anna joined in, 'Great idea, Cosima.'

Demitrius found himself unable to break Cosima's gaze, as much as he felt he wanted to respond to Anna. He turned his head, but it would not move. Not yet. He smiled at Cosima's brilliant face, so alive in the moonlight, so filled with youth, until she looked to Anna and nodded.

'Anna,' she called out, 'it's a good idea, no? Isn't it?'

Demitrius glanced over his shoulder to Stefano, who simply smiled and shrugged his shoulders.

'Yes, sure we can go for a little ride,' Demitrius told them all. 'Let me just get the key.' With that he left them, entering the house for a moment and then appearing again just as swiftly. 'We'll go out and do some whale watching,' he said over his shoulder as he led the way to the pier.

'Whale watching?' Anna cried, then laughed. 'Oh you.' Demitrius turned in his step and smiled at her. 'You had me going for a second there,' she told him.

They all followed Demitrius onto the pier and then into the boat. Cosima came on board last, taking Demitrius's hand as she did. 'Oh!' she said as her toes touched the floor of the boat. She quickly grasped Demitrius's arm as well. 'The floor is moving.' She found her footing, and flashed her white teeth. 'Let's go!'

For Demitrius and Stefano it was all automatic. Stefano untied the boat while Demitrius stood at the wheel and fired up the *Helios*'s engine. Stefano, standing on the pier, pushed out the back end of the boat with his foot and then jogged forward a few steps and did the same to the nose before jumping up lightly onto the side of the boat and then stepping down into her to join Despina and Anna at the bow as they waited for the excitement to begin. Cosima stood next to Demitrius, holding onto the frame of the window of the cabin opposite him and just behind the others. 'Okay,' Demitrius called out, 'Everyone hold on!'

As Demitrius pushed the throttle lever forward the *Helios*'s engine jumped up a notch and they were thrust forward. The women all tightened their grip on whatever it was they were holding onto at the sudden jolt. This lasted for a few moments, before the engine jumped again, bringing them along at an even faster pace, until a third and final jump set the wind to their hair and smiles to their faces as they sped off under the light of the brilliant moon.

The laughter of Demitrius's guests wasn't completely lost to the whine of the engine as the boat sped and bounced along. The thrill of the speed was a surprise to them all as they noted, one by one, that the wine in their blood was adding to the excitement. 'Yeah!' Cosima cried, as Demitrius found her eyes with his and returned her joyful expression. Her hand darted across to him and landed on his arm, feeling his muscle, and the hair on his forearm, before returning to help steady her stance on the speeding boat. She squinted into the wind but her smile remained. Demitrius, checking the horizon quickly to ensure that they had a free path, turned and watched Cosima. He could not understand why, but he felt a kind of longing for her then. He felt that he wanted to take her in his arms and comfort her. But comfort her for what? From what?

He turned and looked forward again, out over the bow of the boat, over the heads of the others as they sat on the low bench seats on either side of the arc of the bow. The way was clear. It was plain to see. He watched Anna as she held onto the rail of the boat. He was glad for the opportunity to bring her into his world, if only in this way, for a pleasure trip. It was not fishing, but they were on his boat, enjoying every second. If people could admire the pieces Anna's husband made, they could also admire the *Helios*, and how it was piloted, and what bounty it could bring back from the sea.

Demitrius checked the gauges on the dashboard automatically. Oil pressure, gasoline, engine speed. Everything was as it should be. He looked up again at the horizon and then turned to Cosima. But this time, he saw that a change had taken place in her expression. Her eyes were still closed, the wind still whipped through her hair. Her lips were pressed together but her smile waned. Or was it not so? Was it only the moonlight making it appear this way? Demitrius kept his eye on Cosima. Then he was sure of it. She was suffering from something but was fighting it, whatever it was. She opened her eyes again and, once more, gave him a smile. Her best effort. But then she closed her eyes and the struggle continued. Demitrius realized she was struggling for him. He saw how she wanted to please him, to enjoy the thrill of his fishing boat despite whatever it was that tormented her. And then Demitrius saw it clearly. Of course, she was feeling sick! Suddenly Cosima's eyes shot open and her hand went to her head.

Demitrius immediately brought the engine to half throttle, and then after a moment to an idle as Cosima turned and stepped over to the side of the boat, resting her knees on the gunwale. Demitrius held her around the waste and held her arm as she became sick. Cosima's retching caught everyone's attention.

'Oh, Cosima is feeding the fish!' Stefano cried out.

'Stefano!' Despina snapped, unwrapping his arm from around her shoulders and placing it roughly in his lap.

Anna was at Cosima's side in an instant, taking hold of her while Demitrius quickly retrieved a jug of water and filled the cup of his hand with it, holding it to Cosima's lips as she bent over the shimmering water. 'There you are my dear,' he said to her.

Cosima shut her eyes tightly and began to sob as she fought with the paralyzing effects of the alcohol enhanced seasickness. Demitrius gathered more water from the jug in the palm of his hand and gently rinsed Cosima's face with the cool water.

'Thank you,' Cosima said, 'I'm sorry.'

'Are you feeling better, Cosima?' Anna asked. Then she turned to Demitrius. 'Do you have a cup?' she asked him quietly. He nodded and stood, retrieving a cup from a cabinet and filling it, then handing it to Anna. A moment later Demitrius took Cosima to the bow of the boat and sat with her on one of the bench seats while Stefano turned the boat around and headed back, slowly. 'Cosima,' he told her, 'I know you'll think I'm joking, but I'm not. I'm glad you got us out of the house and into the *Helios*. I'm glad you showed us this beautiful moonlight.'

Cosima looked at him briefly, then closed her eyes again. 'I ruined everything for your guest.'

'What? Nonsense!' Demitrius cried, giving Anna a wink. 'Anna is a big girl. She's not at all bothered, believe me.'

When they arrived back at the pier, Lisa was waiting for them.

In the morning, Demitrius woke to the sound of a car that had driven down his dead-end road, stopped in front of his home, turned around, and slowly drove away again. He probably would have continued sleeping if the driver hadn't accidentally bumped the horn when turning around. He opened his eyes and took a deep breath as thoughts began to fly. The weather, *Helios*, Anna...Cosima! He sat up in bed and put his feet on the floor. Cosima! Anna had told him, or rather had reminded him, of Cosima's feelings for him. He had said that this was not interesting to him. But now, it was! Something had happened, but what, exactly? He shook his head, then tossed the bed covers aside and strode towards the door. Pushing the door open, he stepped outside and had a look around as he did every morning of every day. Must be about eleven, he thought. He looked at his boat, remembering that he and Stefano had taken her out in the middle of the night. She was still there. Good. Cosima! The sunlight hurt his eyes and his head. He went back inside to the bathroom and shaved without turning on the light. He showered and hoped that coffee would help make the world understandable again.

With shaving cream hiding inside his ears he put on his sandals and walked over to the little house, his old house, to see what Anna was up to. As he arrived outside the door he heard her voice. She was talking to someone inside the house. He stopped, thinking she must be speaking to her husband on her cell phone. But by the way she spoke he could tell that it was to someone who was there, in the house with her. Surprised and, somehow, disappointed, he knocked on the door. He would find out who she was with. But instead of an embarrassed silence followed by panicked scrambling, he was invited inside. He frowned, then opened the door he had opened for so many years, every day. As he opened the door he felt something against his leg and looked down to see Lisa, the goat, looking up at him inside the house.

'Hi, good morning Demitrius,' Anna called from the table where she sat with her notebook and coffee. 'Lisa has been keeping me company. Come in, come in,' she beckoned, smiling at him as he stepped inside with an expression that said *I hope your hangover is manageable.*

'Good morning Anna,' Demitrius said as he entered the old house. He looked down at Lisa, who stood at his knee looking at him. 'Well, in or out Lisa, what do you want?' Lisa rubbed his leg with her head and then ran outside, very quickly, for about two seconds before stopping just as suddenly and putting her mouth onto a tuft of grass and chewing at it, her tail twitching behind her. 'Okay, out she goes,' Demitrius said as he turned to Anna and took a seat at the table opposite her. 'Anna, I see you've got the coffee going. Have you eaten yet?' Anna closed her notebook and smiled the biggest smile Demitrius had seen on her face since they met. Surprised, he looked at the notebook and pointed. 'Is the writing going well?'

'Oh, Demitrius, you have no idea,' she began. 'You know, last night I told the truth, but I lied as well.'

Demitrius cocked his head. 'Yes? Well, tell me more.'

'I have a confession to make,' Anna said, drawing her breath and her hands together, clutching them at her chest and then shaking her head and laughing. 'It's gone! It's really gone! And I owe it all to you and Cosima and Stefano and Despina. I have to thank you all, really, from the bottom of my heart.'

'Gone?' Demitrius asked, failing completely to comprehend what it was that Anna was talking about.

'My writer's block. Yes.'

'Writer's block?'

Anna nodded, then a look of grave seriousness crossed her face and she leaned forward over the table at Demitrius. 'My goodness, Demitrius, yes. Writer's block. With a capital 'B' in fact.' She shrugged her shoulders and shivered and then smiled warmly once again. 'I have been suffering from writer's block for about a year now.'

'What?' Demitrius asked, sitting back in his chair and putting the palms of his hands flat on the table.

'You know, it happens to writers from time to time. They just can't find anything anymore. The well dries up. They try to write but nothing comes. No good ideas. Nothing that pleases them. It's a terrible affliction, let me tell you. Because you want to write, you still feel an urge to do this thing, but...nothing comes. It's awful.' Anna sat for a moment gazing into the space between them, her expression blank. 'Well, anyway, let me explain. Last night, when you all started asking me about what it was that I was writing about, well, I had nothing to say, you see? Nothing! Because I was not writing anything!'

'Oh,' Demitrius said. 'I see.'

'Yes. But I could not tell you that. It would have been embarrassing, so...well, I bluffed. Well no, first, I panicked. I panicked and my mind was racing and I was trying to come up with something to say, and then I made a kind of bluff I think – I don't remember now so well exactly what I said, but – and then, my god, your wonderful goat Lisa came rubbing up against me and POW!'

'Really?'

'Yes! I looked down at her and started to pet her and she looked at me with these eyes with so much expression behind them and suddenly, I knew what I had to write about. I knew I had to write about Lisa the goat.'

Demitrius could hardly believe it. His mouth fell open and he waited for Anna to give up and tell him that she was only joking. Only, she did not do any such thing. 'No,' he told her. 'Come on.'

'It's the truth,' Anna said. She was clearly very happy. Demitrius had to believe her. He told her that he was happy that she was able to work out her writer's block on Naxos. Then he suggested that they head over to his house for breakfast.

As they ate bread and eggs and drank more coffee Anna told Demitrius that she would like to go out on the boat again. He agreed. It was Saturday. He wasn't planning to work. He had more than enough time. She told him that the feeling of being on the sea was, unfortunately, cut short the night before due to Cosima's seasickness and that she wanted ever so much to be out again on the open ocean.

'It will be my pleasure,' Demitrius told her. 'And in fact, it is a good thing that you ask. I am looking forward to the same thing, myself.' He did not explain to Anna that he needed to be on the water because he had some thinking to do, but it was just so. The sea was where he liked to solve his problems, to let his mind work out the puzzles of life. He had a puzzle now. After breakfast they put some things together to eat and drink and then met on the pier. Anna brought her camera and a hat to guard against the sun. Demitrius had everything else they would need. They headed out to the *Helios* and as they reached the ropes that held her fast to the pier the clippity-clop of Lisa's hooves sounded behind them as she raced down the pier and collided gamely with Demitrius's leg.

'Hey girl,' Demitrius called to her. 'You want to put me into the water, eh? You funny girl.'

'Oh, Demitrius, can we bring Lisa along too?' Anna asked, feeling warmth swell up inside her for the little beast that was now soothing the itch inside her.

Demitrius was about to laugh out loud and dismiss the idea out of hand, and then, he thought to himself, *How will I explain the reason why not?* And then he realized there was no reason why not, there was only the prejudice against such an idea. 'Well, of course,' he told her. 'Why not, after all? Yes! We'll bring her along.'

'Marvelous!' Anna cried. 'You know, Lisa is now my muse, so I feel as if I just have to have her everywhere with me. I suppose you think it's silly,' she said as she stepped into the *Helios* and turned to watch as Demitrius picked Lisa up in his arms. He stopped and looked at Anna.

'No, I don't think it's silly,' he said, then stepped into the boat carefully before setting Lisa down. He stood upright and placed his hands on his hips, then crossed his arms over his chest. 'Now,' he said to Lisa, who stood very still while she gathered in the movement of the earth under her feet, 'you behave yourself, little goat.' Demitrius untied the lines fore and aft and started the engine while Anna took a place at the bow and prepared herself. She was thrilled that Lisa had taken a seat on the bench just opposite her, all on her own, as if she knew that this ride was for two girls out looking for some fun. This time, Demitrius piloted the *Helios* at a slower pace than the night before, but it was still fast enough to give Anna the feeling of getting away from something, or of rushing out to somewhere. She turned and smiled at Demitrius as the sun shone down upon them and the boat passed easily over the calm sea. They continued on for a good quarter of an hour before Demitrius slowed the *Helios* and then shut her engine off, allowing them to drift. The sea was calm and there was only a slight breeze blowing over the water. Enough to bring some comfort from the sun but not enough to move the waves or the *Helios*. Peaceful, calm, quiet. Demitrius had baited a line and flung it out into the water shortly after they had stopped, locking the fishing pole in a stand at the stern and leaving the bait to do its work. The fisherman in him couldn't allow him to be there without trying to bring something home for dinner.

He and Anna sat together in the bow of the boat on the comfortable padded seats without saying a word for a long time, while Lisa had escaped the direct sunlight in favor of the shade under the steering wheel in the cabin. It was good for both of them, to just sit and think. Anna of her work, and of the story that was developing in her mind. Demitrius was also occupied with the curiosities of life and love. He thought about his life until that point in its entirety, from his first memories, to life as a boy, to his teenage years and beyond. For many years he had given up on the search for love. Or rather, it had escaped him, like a lover slipping quietly out from the bed early in the morning, leaving him alone and unaware of being alone. Now the urge was back. Of course he had known about the way Cosima felt about him, but it hadn't mattered to him before. Why not? He realized that it had only been until Anna arrived that he had started having thoughts of the long life alone that he had been living. But was it only because he had been asked to tell the story of his life, yesterday, while he and Anna sipped wine and prepared dinner? Somehow he knew it was not so simple. No, it was Anna herself that had prompted this change. She had appeared before him, dangled like a shiny lure. The desire for love that was thus awakened in him had to be answered. He knew it could not be answered by Anna, but he had not expected it to take the course it seemed now to have taken.

It was with the thought of the lure that Anna had been to him still on his mind, when he felt her hand upon his hand.

'Demitrius,' Anna said, looking to the stern of the *Helios* and pointing with her other hand, 'your fishing pole is moving.'

Demitrius looked up and was on his feet instantly. He could see plainly that there was a fish on the line. How long had it been there? He cursed himself for having lost himself in his thoughts and failing to monitor the line. The pole was bent at a sharp angle and was dancing around madly. Whatever it was, it was big. The *Helios* was a commercial fishing boat but Demitrius had outfitted her stern with one simple sport fishing chair, both for his own use and for taking tourists out on lucrative day-trips. 'Okay, you fish, let's get you in,' he said as he sat down on the chair next to where his pole was locked into place. He sat down and fastened a belt that was attached to the chair around his waist so that he could not be pulled bodily out of it. He unlocked the pole and then took it up, placing the butt end of it into the holder between his legs. He looked out into the water, following where the line lead and disappeared, into the deep.

There were a few sharp, powerful tugs on the line, followed by a lapse that felt odd. Very odd, in fact. Then followed only a gentle pulling, or so it felt after such power had been on display. What is this? Anna watched from where she sat at the bow, unbeknownst to Demitrius, who now scanned the water left and right. And then he saw it. The shark's dorsal fin broke the surface of the water, followed by the tip of its tail. 'No,' Demitrius said. Then he shouted. 'Thief! You bastard!'

'What is it?' Anna asked him. 'What's wrong?' She stood then and went to the cabin and held onto the edge of the roof above the steering wheel.

'A shark got my fish,' Demitrius told her as he reeled in the line that no longer fought back.

'A shark?' Anna cried, alarmed at the word. 'Are there sharks here?' She felt a bit foolish having asked the question.

'Yes, but they're rare. Normally they're farther out, but in any case, they're rare. And this one, he was big. Big for the Mediterranean at least. Two meters, I'd say.'

Anna felt her grip tighten on the wood of the cabin. 'You mean you saw it?'

'The shark? Yes. He surfaced a minute ago for a second.'

'What happened?'

'Well, I wasn't paying attention,' Demitrius admitted, 'The fish was on the line and of course started panicking and that attracted the shark. I don't know how long he was on the line before you saw the fishing pole moving.' At that, he unclipped his belt and stood up from the chair. He raised the pole up and brought the remains of a large fish into the boat, letting it down on the deck. 'Well, that would have been nice,' he said as he stowed the pole and removed the hook from the mouth of the fish with a pliers. He stood and held the remains up for a moment for Anna to see, shrugging his shoulders before tossing the poor bounty back to the sea. Anna smiled apologetically. This was not her world. A large fish had been lost to them to a shark. She was not sure how Demitrius felt about it. Perhaps he was more upset than he was letting on. She allowed her gaze to travel over the steering wheel, over the gauges, as Demitrius put the pliers away and rinsed his hands in a bucket and then dried them on a towel that hung on the wall of the cabin.

'Oh!' Anna cried softly, then whispered to Demitrius. 'Demitrius, come look! Look at Lisa.' Demitrius came to her and stopped at her side. Anna pointed at Lisa, who lay at her feet, curled up under the steering wheel, asleep. 'Look,' Anna whispered again. 'Look at her feet. She's dreaming!' The hooves of the goat twitched and trembled.

Demitrius laughed. 'She's chasing her lover.'

Anna turned to Demitrius in surprise. 'You think so?'

Anna turned and went back to the cushioned seat at the bow. Demitrius followed silently. They sat and surveyed the sea, both of them sighing heavily. Moments later, a sound caught their attention and they turned to see Lisa standing in the cabin looking shocked, as if she had just been transported there from some far off place and time. Bewildered, she turned around once, then stood stiffly. Anna and Demitrius both smiled at her.

'Lisa, you're awake,' Anna called out.

'Maybe she's hungry,' Demitrius said. 'I forgot to bring something for her.'

Before either of them had a chance to stop her, Lisa ran to the stern and placed her front hooves up on the gunwale, looking out at the water. She looked left, then right, and then suddenly hopped up and plunged into the deep. Demitrius and Anna immediately shot up and went to where Lisa had jumped. The silence was then broken as Lisa surfaced, not far from the boat but out of reach, her hooves cutting the water as she splashed, able to swim but at the moment having no direction in mind. Demitrius and Anna called out to her, their arms extended, reaching. Then Lisa began swimming determinedly, away from the boat and out to sea.

Anna stood up straight with a look of shock on her face. 'The shark.'

'Where?' Demitrius asked.

'I don't know, but he's out there somewhere isn't he?' Demitrius went to grab a gaff while Anna bent over the gunwale once more and pleaded with Lisa. 'Lisa, my dear, please come back!'

And then, as if she had hear Anna's pleas and understood them perfectly, Lisa made an abrupt about face and began swimming directly to the boat. Anna cried tears of joy as she and Demitrius received Lisa, pulling her into the *Helios*. Lisa stood still on the deck of the boat in their arms, but then broke free. She ran to the center of the boat and stopped again abruptly as she so often did, standing stock still. Anna wrapped her arms around the Lisa and called out to Demitrius for a towel to dry her with. Demitrius retrieved a towel and the two of them dried Lisa, stroked her fur, and spoke to her. Then Demitrius stopped and sat on his knees in the middle of the boat as Anna continued to dry Lisa, who had by then sat down where she stood and laid her head on the deck.

'Anna,' Demitrius said, reaching out and taking Anna by the hand for just a moment before letting her hand go again. 'Anna, I wanted it to be you.' He waited until she made eye contact with him, then he dropped his gaze to the floor of the boat.

'What?' Anna asked him.

'I wanted it to be you,' Demitrius continued. Then his expression of grave seriousness slipped into an embarrassed grin. 'As if it could have been you.' His eyes searched her face. 'You, the married woman.'

Anna stopped drying Lisa. Lisa looked at her, then rose quietly and stepped away, wandering to the bow of the boat before laying down again and turning back to look at them. Anna turned to face Demitrius. 'Tell me.'

'I wanted it, somehow, to be you. But now, it is Cosima.' Demitrius laughed once. 'Now, it is Cosima. And I cannot believe it, and it makes me sad. As if I lost you. As if I could lose you. But I am...' But he had no words. He simply watched Anna. He smiled. Anna saw his look and returned it.

'You look happy, Demitrius!'

'Yes! That's just it. I am!'

'You're happy. Somehow, you found Cosima.'

Demitrius shrugged. 'Yes, in fact. That's exactly it.' He shook his head and shrugged again.

'You don't need to apologize or to feel sad.'

'No. I don't, do I?'

Anna watched him, then stood and offered him her hand. 'No, you don't.'

The three of them sat in the bow of the *Helios*. Anna explained once again how much she was enjoying the story she started. They ate the food they brought, and drank cold orange juice. Anna told Demitrius that she would like to try fishing the next day, if that would be okay. Demitrius agreed happily. 'But Lisa will stay at home,' he said. With that, he rose, started the boat's engine and set a course for home.

As the house and the pier finally became visible, Anna felt relief. Then she noticed a figure standing on the pier. Demitrius saw it too. The *Helios* powered smoothly on. It was a man. A man, and a goat, standing on the pier, waiting for them. 'John?' Anna spoke out loud, bringing her hand to her lips. She smiled. 'It's John. It's my husband, John!'

'And he has a goat with him!' Demitrius cried. Sure enough, Anna's husband stood at the end of the pier with his hand resting on the head of a billy goat standing at his side.

'Yes,' Anna said. She crouched down next to Lisa who stood next to her. 'Lisa my love, do you see? Do you see?'

* * *

I could not believe it when I saw my man standing on the pier with Anna's man. Just before, I had been running with him on a hill with wonderful green grass. I had stopped and my heart felt so full that I cried out to him 'Now you don't go away anymore, do you understand me?' And he stopped too, because he could see that I was serious. And he agreed not to leave me again, ever. But then, there I was on the *Helios* with Anna and Papi and my man was nowhere! He had promised, but he was gone. He wouldn't do that, is what I thought, so I thought that maybe he had fallen into the water. I looked but could not find him, so I did what any other goat would do. I jumped in to rescue him. And when I was in the water I heard him say to me 'No! Not here! I am not here! Get back into the *Helios* and go home!' And so I did. I felt fine when I was back on board because my man had told me. So I knew it would be okay.

Then we arrived and Papi tied up the *Helios*. My man looked so handsome! I jumped out as soon as I could and stood by his side. Anna got out too and gave her man a big hug and a kiss. 'The conference was cancelled,' he told her. 'And where did you find this handsome devil?' she asked him. So he told her: 'I met him on the road and he followed me here. He's a beauty, isn't he?' And he was. Anna was so happy. She introduced Papi to her man and they liked each other right away. Then she told him about her writing, and that she was writing about me! I had to give her a kiss then. And then, finally, my man and I left them. 'Now don't you ever leave me,' I told him. He smiled and kissed me. 'No, never,' he said. And he has never left since then.

A long road to good-bye

I remember exactly how it came about that I got it into my head that I absolutely had to say goodbye to Nancy Winters before she and her family moved back to Virginia. It was a long time ago, but I haven't forgotten. I must have been only fourteen. A freshman in high school in Southern Germany, where we lived for a short time. It was summertime. I remember that it had been really hot then, abnormally so. When I woke up that Saturday morning to find it raining outside, and I mean really pouring, I couldn't believe it. What had happened to all the sun? How on earth could it be raining? Especially on that day.

Then I remembered that the night before, my mother had said it was supposed to rain. She had told me, but I of course didn't believe her. I woke up early, had my breakfast, and left. I told my mother that I was riding my bike to the base to meet some friends. I didn't do that often. I'm American. I grew up being driven everywhere. The Germans were like that too, I learned. They loved their cars, just like Americans. Liked to drive everywhere, when they could just have easily taken a train. Not so easy in the States, but in Germany they have much better public transportation. But still. They loved their cars.

That Saturday, my parents had no intention of going to the base. I had to get there on my own. It was four or five miles to the base, which seemed like a huge distance to me.

Although I hadn't really realized how far it was until I started off, hoping my rain jacket would keep the rain out. Keeping my head down against the steady pelter of cold wetness all around me. The main roads between our village and the army base had no bike lanes. I rode through the meandering street that cut through our little village, past the bäckerei, past the shop selling motorcycles and lawnmowers, past the butcher. My pants were soaked at my thighs before I even escaped our own village. My resolve took a hit when I realized that. Feeling the cold seeping into my muscles and the wetness of the Levis clinging to me. But then I formed a picture of Nancy in my mind and found the strength to keep going.

I saw her as she was the night before, when we were all at the base watching a softball game. It was another warm, summer night. We were at the lower field, near the entrance of the base. The smell of freshly cut grass hung in the air. And beer. Always beer, at these games. The green of the field was matched by the leafy elm trees that lined the back of the field, near the wall of the base. The field lights had been turned on, although there was still a lot of daylight left in the sky that was rimmed with gold at this time. All the kids were there, but we weren't playing. The adults were playing. Two of the four teams that the small base had put together. My dad was on one of the teams that were playing that night. I had just watched the second baseman catch a fly ball my dad had hit over the pitcher's head, and felt a tremor of shame at the sight of him jogging back along the baseline to get back to his dugout and his teammates. Like me, he was an athletic person but not great in sports, however that worked. I was standing near the bleachers with Eric, my big goofy friend, and a group of other kids, plus a few of the German kids from the village across the street who we knew and liked.

And suddenly Nancy appeared at my side and put her hand on my arm. Her hand was a bit sweaty. We all had a sheen of moisture on us, with the summer heat and our hyperactivity combining to guarantee that. Still, her sudden touch was so sticky warm. I looked at her hand. I knew immediately it was a girl touching me. Other kids probably wouldn't have reacted the way I did, but I was way behind them. Had never really kissed a girl before. I felt this heat and then a tingle in my body, and then suddenly I was looking into her eyes as she stood at my side. Nancy Winters. The girl that I had already measured and placed in the scrap heap in my mind where all of the rejects like her went, in my lunatic boyhood fantasy requiring an impossible perfection from any girl I would ever consider allowing to come near me. It was easier that way. A lot easier than admitting that half of them were cute enough for you to want to kiss them. Nancy's eyes threw bolts of energy into mine that raced through my body and found the heat from her hand and spread it through me like an electric shock.

'Wasn't that your dad?' she asked me, the beauty of her mouth and teeth undeniable. My God. What did you say? How beautiful are you, anyway? She looked toward the field then, after I failed to respond visibly to her question other than to allow my mouth to hang open as if trying to catch some of the fireflies that they had there, but which I had never seen before, growing up in California where I had. I snapped out of it.

'What?' I asked her, and followed her gaze. I saw my dad and then replayed her question in my mind. 'Oh! Yeah, right. Pop fly.'

Nancy looked at me again, her smile even wider than before.

'That was a great hit!'

I smiled, inspecting her lips. And I knew it then, or rather, I remembered. I had always thought she was cute. 'Cute' was what it had been. Not allowed to enter the ranks of the 'pretty,' let alone the 'desirable.' But there she was, looking like a very desirable young teenaged girl to me. Sure, she was a little short. Maybe a little bit overweight. She didn't have long, slender legs and all of those other so-called 'classic' bits of beauty. She had a nice face, and full lips, and freckles, too. Not a whole swarm of them. Not a freckle storm, but nice freckles that contrasted slightly with the surrounding skin. I had no clue at all about haircuts. Hers was on the short side, just brushing her shoulders. But her hair itself, its color and fullness, were actually lovely. But I had rejected her.

Then she said something that blew right through me.

'So, are you going to give me a goodbye kiss before we leave?'

I continued to just stare at her, lost. I don't think I even knew that she and her family were leaving that summer.

You have to understand that in the thirteen-odd months that I had been living there, for our scheduled eighteen-month trip, I had probably not said more than ten words to Nancy Winters. I was a freshman in high school. She was in eighth grade, so we didn't go to the same school. I saw her here and there pretty often. My dad wasn't military, which was why we lived off of the base, whereas Nancy's dad was in the military, so they lived on the base where all the military families lived. But still, we were at the base all the time. That was where we maintained contact with 'back home,' with Americans and the American way of life, even though on that base it was an oddly uniform, white buildings only, rather sterile world, where one could see green army vehicles and green-clothed army types here and there. It certainly didn't look like any picture of home to me, but the culture and the language and all of my new friends were there.

I knew Nancy Winters, but a goodbye kiss? Where had she dreamed that up? Why? I guess then, immediately, I realized that she must have been one of the small handful of girls who had chosen me to be the one, or perhaps one of the ones, more likely, that she had a crush on. As crushes went. Those silent creatures that you never hear about until it's too late to do anything about them. I knew that I was one of the lucky few young guys who were supposed to be good-looking guys, pimples and all, and... Well. A lot of good that did me. The problem was, of course, I had no idea what to do, and I had no courage whatsoever even if I thought I might want to do something.

And this was the difference between other kids and me. Nancy Winters, having reached the ripe age of thirteen, had been able to march up and ask me for a kiss. Because she wanted to. For her, a kiss was just a kiss. Something normal. Something you did. For me, a kiss existed only in the realm of the conceptual. The purely theoretical. Theoretical physics, theoretical kissing. It's all the same.

I figured all this out while the bubblegum smell of Nancy Winters's breath hung in the air in front of my face. And then she did something that knocked me a bit further out of the solar system. She shifted her weight onto one leg and placed her hands on her hips. Yes, without using her voice, she was asking me again. But even more, she had just turned a question into a dare. Hands on hips. Butt out. Come on. Are you going to give it to me, or what?

'Sure,' I said.

Nancy smiled. And waited.

I smiled. I wondered what she was waiting for. Oh. You mean, now? Instantly I felt an ocean-sized pressure swarming over me. Kiss her! Now!

But I guess I had lived fourteen years already without having kissed a girl and wasn't about to change that. The ocean wasn't big enough to force me to do what I knew I wanted, with teenage boy desperation, to do. What I had been asked to do. What was hanging in the air, awkwardly, awaiting birth.

And then I knew that by having waited longer than an instant, I had missed my chance. If I had kissed her now, the long pause would have been the new item for inspection. No. I had to make it sound like I meant to do that.

'Sure,' I told her again, with no plan in mind, but intent on buying some more time.

Nancy chewed her gum once. Twice.

'Okay,' she said, standing up a bit straighter, almost imperceptibly so, and then flouncing back into her pose. Butt out, watch it!

If this was a game, she was playing it, and creaming me. A total smear.

'When are you leaving?' I asked her. I had hatched a brilliant plan. Now, I could delay giving her that kiss until they left. I would have plenty of time to figure out how, when and where to do it. I would have plenty of time to review kissing techniques – with my imagination, of course, as always. And I would have plenty of time to manufacture the courage needed. First I would build the courage factory, then I would start manufacturing. It was a great plan, and I had thought it up all by myself.

Sometimes, I was a genius.

Nancy smiled. 'Tomorrow afternoon,' she said.

Sometimes, even genius fails. Sometimes, even the minds of geniuses fail to consider the correct range of possibilities when they make their plans, based on assumptions as well as on hard facts.

Tomorrow afternoon. Okay. As short as it was, that still left me some time.

By then, Nancy had certainly surmised that I wasn't about to plant one on her in the next few minutes, but she seemed intent on getting what she asked for enough to offer me some more details.

'We're leaving before lunchtime for the airport. We're staying at the BQs now,' she said. BQs being 'bachelor's quarters' which was a row of small apartments meant for soldiers who lived alone, and which also doubled as a temporary living accommodation for arriving or departing families.

No sooner had her words left her lips than my friend Eric called my name.

'Tom!'

I turned my head automatically. Eric was in run-ready mode, motioning me with his arm to follow, a big grin on his face that meant mischief. A few of the other guys were in front of him, loping across the road through the stand of pines that stood between the baseball diamond and the little movie theater we called the Kino.

'We're gonna sneak into the Kino! Come on!'

That was my ticket out of there. I turned back to Nancy, knowing full well that I had just been saved and feeling quite relieved and grateful for it, and then I uttered something that proves that the brain and the mouth don't always work in concert. I raised my pointed finger at Nancy as I started to run after Eric.

'I'll see you tomorrow morning!' I told her. I even remember having had a deadly serious expression on my face as I said it. A look that told her that I was not kidding. I had just given her a *promise*.

Riding my bike through the rain, the question as to why I had to add that little flourish to my getaway the night before was what I thought about next, having left our village behind and turned off onto the shortcut road that ran alongside the border of a few farms before hooking up with a seldom-driven two lane road that headed towards the base. If I hadn't told

Nancy that I would see her tomorrow, I could have just run off, the prisoner of the boy's club, and been off the hook.

I guess I wanted to kiss her. I just needed time to figure myself out.

I kept my head down, and it kept raining on me. I remember then that my bike started to squeak as I settled into a steady rhythm on the long, straight road ahead. A squeak that came with every turn of the cranks, as my right foot gained the top of the arc and came down. I was riding in the rain five miles to the base on my squeaking bike, head tucked down, one eye on the road under the brim of my thoroughly soaked baseball hat that sat under the hood of my rain jacket, to try to find Nancy Winters and kiss her. And it was just then that I realized it: I didn't know where they lived.

Since it was raining, and I wanted to reach my destination and get out of the rain as soon as possible, I'm sure I didn't slow my pace when it hit me that I wasn't sure, exactly, where I was going. I'm sure I kept pumping right along, but my mind started diving left and right.

I was a genius. But even geniuses fail to think of all details. Even simple ones. Even geniuses have been known to set off on a journey without knowing where they were headed. Then I remembered that Nancy had told me that they were staying in the bachelor's quarters at the base. Okay. There were only about four such buildings, each with two floors and maybe twenty units per building. So that narrowed it down. Just then a barking, crazed, black shaggy-haired dog came darting out from one of the farms at my left, headed right for me. I only saw him out of the corner of my eye, the movement creating a reflex reaction in me to turn my head sharply to see what it was. Naturally, this caused me to swerve wildly on the bike as I lost and then regained my balance and kept on pumping, but now with a burst of panic-driven energy. As the dog neared I could see he was an old one. Just as he caught up with me his yapping mouth closed and he looked me in the eye and raised his snout at me as if aiming down the twin barrels of a shotgun. Then he abruptly turned and gave up the chase, content to trot back to his home, victory-barking as he went.

As relief rippled through me I turned at him with new courage and yelled 'Fuck off!' and then instantly felt foolish.

Jesus. I felt the adrenaline running through me then as I continued to pump along, slower now as I turned again to double check that I was in the clear. I couldn't keep the smile of relief from spreading across my face until I saw another dog, in front of me this time, about fifty yards off to the left. It was a German Shepard, no less, moving purposefully towards me in front of a large brick house, his head held high despite the rain, showing perhaps that he was not crazy like the dog before him but was maybe more organized and competent. This time, pedaling faster would just bring me sooner to teeth and jaws. I didn't know what to do, so my body did something for me. Before I knew it I had slowed down and then jumped off the bike, putting the bike between me and the dog. 'I'm just walking my bike through here, man,' I told myself. Giving reasons – maybe to God – why I should be allowed to pass by unmolested. 'Just walking my bike, just trying to get somewhere!'

Then I remembered the eye-contact rule and stopped looking at the dog and looked straight ahead of me instead, marching on, in the rain. I kept putting one foot in front of the other, minding my own business, going my own way, a lover of dogs, actually, all dogs, all animals... Then Mr. Shepard's massive and proud head moved suddenly and I looked to see that he had been alerted to something behind me. I was no longer the focus of his attention. Just then he changed course as well, heading instead towards whatever he had now in his sights. I turned to look and saw the black dog sneaking up behind me, giving me a start and an impulse to jump on the bike again. Just then a loud bark sounded in front of me. I turned and saw the German Shepard start running right towards the other dog. I was on my bike in a flash, pumping for all I was worth, pumping, taking a look back, pumping some more, looking back. I heard some barking and then some hollering and turned to see a woman with thick legs wearing an apron standing in the road looking at the dogs. Pump, pump, pump. Finally, nerves thoroughly rattled, I saw that I was out of danger unless either one of the dogs could drive a car.

All of a sudden I felt a burning sensation in my legs and stopped pedaling as the rain pummeled me mercilessly. I threw my head back and coasted, opening my mouth to grab some cool rainwater, my heart beating madly in my chest. I laughed out loud. I was safe.

I was also approaching the crest of a hill as the land before me began to drop down. The road turned left and then straightened, falling gently. I began picking up speed as I allowed my legs to keep resting. The road settled down and far ahead I could see where it joined the main road. In the distance, cars passed by to the left and to the right, the sound of their engines drowned to me in the rain. Moments later my momentum was checked as the grade flattened. Reluctantly, I put my legs back to work but as soon as I started to put some muscle into it the resistance of the pedals suddenly vanished and my right foot flew off the hard rubber. I looked down to see that the bicycle chain had broken and was now being dragged along the road making a dull leaden scraping sound.

'What the hell?' I said aloud. I hit the brakes and got off the bike and looked at it. 'A broken chain?' I yelled. I had never seen a broken bike chain before. Maybe the master link had just lost its clip? If I could find it, then... But then I looked at the loose ends of the chain and saw it for my own eyes. One link had actually broken. 'Awww, JESUS!' I shouted. Rain was my answer. 'This sucks! I can't...' And then I was speechless. And really mad. In an effort to calm myself I started walking with my pitiful bike towards the main road ahead, as the rain laughed at me. I knew a little about bikes. Back home in California my brother and I rode BMX bikes. We even shared an offroad minibike. My dad had a great shop in the garage and we were always taking things apart. I looked down again at my bike with its broken chain dragging the street and could just see my brother laughing his head off at me as I explained to him that my chain broke. What a stupid and unbelievable circumstance. That's like saying that you were driving your car and the engine fell out of it. Possible, but unheard of. 'Piece of shit,' I said to no one.

Then I came to a tree growing at the roadside. I stopped, looking at it. I walked over to it, leaned my bike against it, and kept right on walking. 'Asshole,' I called out to it as I left.

As I neared the main road a car slowed at my side, just before it was about to enter the road. I turned to look and saw the driver leaning forward, looking at me through the closed passenger door window. Man, big mustache, rain jacket. The window slid down. The man uttered something in German, a language which I had not yet learned. I imagined he was asking me if I needed help, or if I would like a ride with him.

'Do you speak English?' I asked him. His smile faltered and he shook his head. 'Nein,' he said. My shoulders dropped. Then I figured that perhaps I could show him where I wanted to go, somehow, and started thinking of the possibilities. I wanted to go to the American army base. How could I show him that? Then I had an idea: I saluted, and then pretended to be shooting a gun. Not into his face, of course, but at some imaginary target. 'Pchew, pchew, pchew!' I cried, then looked at his reaction to see if he was getting it. His eyes went wide and he frowned and drove away. As I watched him turning right and heading down the main road in the direction I needed to go, I realized that I could have simply told him the name of the village that the army base was in.

'Oh, stupid!' I cried. 'Shit!'

Reaching the main road, I began walking along its shoulder towards the base, listening and watching for cars coming so that I could hitch a ride. Sure enough, it wasn't long before a few cars came along. Of course, with no place to pull over, no car with other cars close behind would bother to try. I watched as three cars came and went. Not only didn't they stop, but they were going pretty fast. It was only a two-lane road with a small shoulder. I moved off the pavement into the grass and continued walking in the grass. In a moment, a couple more cars came along. One of them honked as they went by. People don't walk on this road, I thought to myself. 'What the hell am I doing?'

Just then I looked and saw a car coming in the distance and had a shock. It was a police car. Out of instinct, my arms went wide and I ducked, my legs telling me to run the hell out of there. And where would I go? I looked around quickly. I was standing in the middle of acres and acres of grass, with a road running through it. There was nowhere to run. I turned to look at the approaching police car and thought of my dad. Fuck! He's going to kill me!

The blue lights on the police car turned as the car pulled completely off the road before me. The passenger window slid down. I felt a wave of relief sweep over me. Maybe I wouldn't end up in jail after all. I went over to the window and looked in.

'What are you doing walking za street?' the very annoyed police man asked me – in English, even.

'Can you take me to the army base?' I asked him. Then I remembered my bike. 'My bicycle chain broke,' I said, turning then and pointing to the tree which stood a couple of hundred yards off.

'Zis is very dangerous!' the man said. 'Get in!'

I got in the car. He looked in his side-view mirror and we took off quickly. He hit a switch on the dashboard then. Nothing happened. I figured it must have been for the lights on top of the car.

'Where do you live?' he asked me, not taking his eyes off of the road in front of him.

'In Brookmule,' I told him.

He nodded. 'Brook-moel,' he corrected. 'You cannot walk on zis street. It is very dangerous. Do your parents know you do zis?'

I shook my head. 'No. I mean, they know I'm going to the base, but they don't know that my chain broke. My bike chain broke. That's why I was walking,' I told him. He was about thirty years old and wore a thick brown mustache and, like every policeman in the world it seems, he looked like a policeman, somehow. It had nothing to do with his uniform, which I hadn't even noticed, until then. He wore a white shirt. But then I saw that it, too, somehow, looked like a police white shirt. I started wondering how that could be when he spoke again.

'You like Chair-moni?'

I was caught. No, I don't like living here in this country where I left all of my friends behind and I feel completely strange and lost and helpless sometimes and I can't understand what's on television...

'Yes!' I lied. 'I do.'

'What do you like?' he asked, turning his head and looking me right in the eye for a moment before turning his gaze back to the road.

I felt the heat on the back of my neck as I struggled to find something to say.

'I'm trying to think of the German word,' I told him. Jesus. Brilliant.

'Okay' he said. I realized then how flat and unemotional his voice was. Suddenly I had the feeling I was being tricked. Maybe he wasn't taking me to the base at all. Maybe he was taking me to the police station. Maybe I was completely screwed after all.

'Beer,' I blurted out. In fact, I couldn't stand the taste of beer. Any beer. My eyes opened wide. I remembered then that the drinking age was sixteen. I was fourteen and looked fourteen. I turned ever so slightly to see what kind of thoughts he might be thinking about me just admitting that what I seemed to like the most about living in Chair-moni was breaking the law. The policeman was nodding. Nodding, and smiling.

'Yes,' he said. 'It's the best.' Then he took a deep breath and seemed to relax.

I made it. I wasn't going to jail now, I was sure of it. He turned and smiled at me, then watched the road again. YES! I really was okay.

'Why are you going to the army base?' He asked, casually. I felt it an odd question, but then I figured he was maybe just trying to make conversation. Again, I wondered what to say. Should I tell the truth, or something else?

'To kiss a girl,' I said. I looked at him and he smiled again, then he laughed.

'Beer and kissing girls,' he said. 'You're a good boy!'

Suddenly, I liked this policeman, more or less. Except for the mustache.

'Don't tell your parents about zis. It will only make zem mad. But don't do it again,' he said as he turned left off of the main road. We were very close to the base now. The rain hadn't let up one bit. I started thinking about how I could get home without asking for help from my parents and realized I probably wouldn't be able to.

The policeman turned left again, into the entrance of the base which had a gate and a checkpoint which looked to be unmanned at the moment. He stopped the car and nodded.

'Okay, this is the end,' he said. He was looking at me and smiling. It seemed to me that he was looking at me as if he had just told a joke and was waiting to see if I got it.

'Thanks,' I told him. I opened the door and got out of the car. Before I closed the door I turned to look at him and saw that he wanted to say something. I put my head back inside out of the rain.

'Hey,' he said, 'I love ze Doors!'

I hesitated.

'Jim Morrison,' he said.

'Oh, yeah,' I said. Then I lied again. 'Me too.'

The policeman turned around and drove off. I quickly ran just inside the gate and entered the MP's office. If the checkpoint wasn't manned, you still had to stop in at the MP's office to let them know who you were. I went inside and the policeman on duty recognized me. He nodded. I was allowed to go in.

I pulled my hood a bit tighter over my baseball hat and started jogging to the bachelor's quarters. As I sloshed along through the rain in thoroughly wet clothes, I realized I hadn't really thought at all about my plan.

I needed a plan, after all. I couldn't just show up and say 'Here I am,' and give Nancy Winters a kiss, I thought to myself. Or could I? How would this even work? I would knock on their door and her mother would answer and...what was I going to do? 'Hello, I'm here to kiss Nancy quickly before you all leave.' Is that what I would say? What if her father answered the door? I fought the impulse to stop running so that I could think things over. 'I need to get out of the rain to think things over,' I told myself, and ran faster.

I reached the BQs a minute later and ducked into the first one. It was a two-storey building. Smaller than the apartment houses on the base. I sat down on the steps inside the building as soon as I entered. The first floor was up one small flight of stairs from the entrance. A door to the right of the entrance held a staircase just inside it that led straight down to the basement. The basements of all the BQs were connected. One common thrill we kids participated in was the exploration of the labyrinth of underground passageways connecting many of the buildings on the base.

Sitting on the steps I happened to look up on the wall to my right and saw a directory of apartments in the building. 'Donovan – 10, Miller – 11, Brown – 12,' it read. I jumped up, realizing that my job had hopefully just gotten a lot easier, assuming that every apartment was included in the list, even for the temporary tenants like Nancy and her family. I started reading the list from the beginning, slowly, as if the gods would reward me for being patient. 'Donovan – 10, Miller – 11, Brown – 12, Winters – 13.'

Holy shit. They were here, in the first floor!

I sat down again on the steps, then I realized that they could come walking in or out, or right behind my back, at any moment. I stood up and opened the door to the basement and let it close behind me on its automatic hinge. The stairs and corridor below were lit. I went to the bottom of the stairs and sat down. I had to have a plan.

As I started to try to get my mind into sneaky mode for thinking about things like this, I realized that there wasn't much for me to plan at all. I had to go to the door and knock on it. After that…okay, so that's where the plan starts. What to say. 'Hi, is Nancy home?' wait till she comes to the door.

Since every plan that began to hatch in my mind started with a knock on the door of the Winters's apartment, I soon changed my tactics. First, I should find the door and have a look at it, then start thinking of a plan. After all, there was no use in figuring out a great plan and then finding out that the directory at the foot of the stairs was somehow wrong. That the Winters actually weren't staying here.

I stood up and walked down the brightly lit hallway to the end of the building and the bottom of the stairway leading up to the ground floor. This stairway was different from the other one. This one had a landing. It was eight steps up to the landing, then a right turn and another eight steps to the hallway. At this end of the building, there was no door to the stairway. As I rounded the landing I froze as I heard a door opening and closing. Footsteps, then another door opening and closing. I began tiptoeing up the last six steps. Were they leaving already? Who was that in the hallway just now? Ahead of me in the hallway I could see that there was no door directly in front of the stairwell. I crept up the last steps and peaked around the corner down the hallway. I saw the door marked thirteen and felt my pulse quicken. I ducked back around the corner and took a deep breath. I looked again and before I knew it, a door on the stairway side of the hallway suddenly opened. My body tensed and I began to jump back until I noticed that the door opened toward me, hiding me from whomever was coming out through it. And that door was closer to me than the door to the Winters's apartment, the last apartment door in the building, so when they started walking, even if it wasn't one of the Winters's, they should walk away from me, with their back to me. I held my breath as I heard a female voice. Whomever had opened the door was standing in the opening and speaking to someone in the room they were leaving. 'And don't take all day, Nancy, you know we have to get going soon.'

Who was that? It wasn't her mother. The voice was too young. As I realized who it must have been I saw Nancy's older sister Diane emerge from the doorway. Then I remembered what must have been behind that door. When my family first arrived, we also stayed in the BQs. I remembered then in a fraction of a second that the apartments didn't have bathrooms. The bathrooms and showers were across the hall. You had to share them with the other people in the apartment. I think there were two of them in each building. As the door began closing behind Diane and she stepped away from it my eyes went wide. Diane was barefoot and had a towel around her waist. She was naked from the waist up. Diane, it must be said, was a senior in our high school and was one of the most attractive and grown up girls too. Naturally, her crowd was not my crowd, but of course I still saw her here and there, regularly, and every time I did I realized how much of a gap there was between her and me. She wasn't even a girl. She was a woman. She and all the other kids her age who were also as...developed, as she was, intimidated me. They were grown-ups who were attending my school! It was one of those high school phenomenon that, being just a freshman and having been from the oldest group in the junior high school that I left behind, freaked me out completely. This created a kind of line between us. You stayed away from them because they intimidated you. They were like your parents, somehow, only they didn't have to be nice or worry about what other people would think if they decided to throw a milkshake at you.

I couldn't believe my eyes. Diane Winters, topless. Right there. Diane walked slowly as she fiddled with her towel, making sure it was properly tucked in or something. My mind was racing. I couldn't believe my luck. But her back was to me. I actually hadn't seen her breasts at all. That would be the question every boy I would ever tell this would immediately ask me. Did you see her tits? Did you? Suddenly I started feeling unlucky. How could being so lucky turn into being unlucky so fast? Diane kept going as she sorted out her towel and was reaching out for the door to their apartment before I knew it. Then she stopped completely and turned toward the door and gave me a beautiful view of her right breast. Then she opened the door and vanished before my eyes.

I disappeared back around the corner and then sat down on a step. My heart was pounding so hard in my chest I seriously thought that maybe I was having a heart attack. I took some deep breaths. I was shaking, my nerves had gotten so worked up. I replayed the scene in my mind and smiled. How lucky was I? I looked out the window on the landing into the rainy gray morning outside and tried to compose myself. Then it occurred to me: what if Nancy came out of the bathroom topless too? My initial excitement turned to reservation as I realized that this was something I didn't really want to see. Diane was a woman. Nancy was a girl. Just a girl. I hadn't even kissed a girl in my life. Seeing Nancy topless was just going too fast. The realization somehow surprised and disturbed me. Was there something wrong with me? Hadn't I always fantasized about seeing the prettiest girls in school without their clothes on? Yes, I admitted to myself then, I had. So what was the problem? Nancy Winters wasn't one of the prettiest girls in school. Actually, she wasn't even in my school. Next year, she would be, or would have been if she weren't leaving, but this year she was still in the eighth grade. She was really just a girl. But last night, I saw something in her that excited me so much that I knew there was something special about her. So why was she different from those other girls? Did she even have breasts? I pictured her in my mind then. Yes, in fact, she did. In fact, for her age, she was rather well developed. So they were real breasts.

So what was wrong with me?

I figured out later that all of this deep philosophy was most likely just my way of avoiding having to think of what the hell I was planning to do.

My plan! I still had none!

'Tom Miller,' I thought to myself, 'the fact is, you're chicken. You're afraid to kiss Nancy Winters, or any other girl, and so you're just going to sit here and let this chance slip through your fingers! Why don't you, for once in your life, just be a man and do what you have to do?'

It was pretty tough talk. It was true, too. Was I listening, though?

I stood up and pursed my lips and turned around, then stepped up into the empty hallway. I glared at the Winters' door. I was ready. Suddenly the bathroom door opened and out came Nancy. Unlike Diane, Nancy was wrapped up tight, wearing a bathrobe, slippers, a towel around her neck and another one wrapped around her head. I stood in the hallway, frozen. I was about to call out her name when I had a thought. What if she would feel embarrassed at me standing there, with her in her bathrobe? Maybe I should wait until she had a chance to get dressed? But that would mean having to knock on the door and raise the attention of everyone in her family. Here, it was just the two of us. Just the way I needed it to be.

I had to make up my mind. She was slipping away. I backed up and retreated down the steps, out of view. I heard the door open and close. I couldn't help feeling like I had let myself down but at the same time I knew it was for the best. I sat down on the steps again and held my head in my hands. I was getting cold. I was wet and cold and hungry. I started thinking of what I would like to eat. I looked up and out the window again. It had stopped raining. Two kids that I recognized from school walked by on the sidewalk outside across the street in front of the building, holding hands. The boy was laughing.

I stood up and walked over to the door. I knocked on it three times, hard enough to be sure that it was heard. I quickly pulled my hood back and removed my baseball cap just as the door opened. In front of me stood Mr. Winters, tall, and expressionless. I recognized him but had never met him before.

'Hello Mr. Winters, is Nancy home?'

Mr. Winters closed his eyes, then reopened them. A slow motion blink if I ever saw one. I looked behind him into the apartment. It was just like ours was when we stayed there.

'Who are you?' he asked me, still no smile, nothing.

'I'm Tom Miller.'

'What,' he said, 'Are you here to kiss her goodbye?'

My mouth fell open and I had one of those thoughts about the amazing ability of parents to know things that they just couldn't know when he smiled and stepped back from the door.

'Just kidding,' he said. He turned. 'Nancy? You've got a visitor.' He motioned for me to come in just as Nancy's mother approached from the kitchen.

'Well, have you come to help us lift some heavy suitcases dear?' she asked me with the same oddly relaxed drawl that her husband had. Southern talk, is what I called it. We didn't really have that in California, but living in this small community of Americans I had come to know a number of people who talked like that. I thought it was cool. Like real live television.

I smiled and shrugged. 'Sure,' I said.

'Nancy's gettin' dressed honey, what's your name?'

'Tom Miller.'

She put out her hand and I took it in mine. 'Well, pleased to meet you Tom. I think I've heard of you.' She smiled at me very sweetly. I couldn't help but like her instantly. 'Nancy'll be out in a minute, honey.' Then she put her hands to her cheeks and her eyes went wide. She looked me up and down. 'Oh, but you're all wet!'

I hadn't even thought about that. My heart started to sink. Would I be ordered to leave?

'Here, let me take that jacket of yours darlin'' she said. 'Go on, give it to me and I'll hang it up.' She took my coat from me and walked back into the kitchen, talking over her shoulder as I watched Mr. Winters surveying a number of open suitcases that lay on the floor directly in front of me in the middle of the living room. 'Are you hungry dear? We just had breakfast, would you like something to eat?'

Yes, I would. 'Oh no, thank you,' I told her.

'Oh, nonsense, you must be starving, coming in here all wet like that. Where do you live, anyway?'

I told her the name of the village where we lived. Mr. Winters turned and stared at me. Mrs. Winters appeared in the doorway of the kitchen, her hands on her hips.

'In Brook-Mule?' she cried. 'What, how did you get here honey, on your bike or somethin''

'Yes,' I told her. I looked at Mr. Winters. He whistled a long whistle and then went back to the luggage.

'Oh, no wonder you're all wet. Here, you just take your shoes off and come in here and sit down. I'm gonna get you something warm in a jiffy.' She stood next to me while I slipped off my shoes and then she ushered me into the kitchen before I could say a word. She pulled out a chair at the kitchen table for me before turning and opening the refrigerator door. 'How about some hot coco and some soup. Would that be okay?' she asked. The way she looked at me, I figured I had better agree to her offer. Besides, it sounded perfect.

'Well, if you're sure it's okay,' I told her. She just waved her hand and hissed.

'My pleasure, dear. Nancy!' she cried, 'Get on out here!'

From where I sat I could look directly through the living room into a doorway that led back to the bedrooms. As I looked into the doorway, Nancy's head popped around the corner. Her eyes were wide. She seemed to be hiding behind the corner. I imagined that she wasn't fully dressed yet. She stared into the room, open-mouthed with surprise. When she spotted me her eyes widened and she smiled.

'I'll be right there,' she called. Just as she did, her sister Diana's head popped around the corner just above hers. She squinted at me and then smiled.

'Didn't know you had a boyfriend, Nance,' she teased. Two heads quickly disappeared again and I shifted my embarrassed gaze to the man of the house. Mr. Winters looked at me and smiled, then took a deep breath and stood up.

'Sweetheart, I'm going to get the car,' he called from where he stood in the living room into the kitchen.

Mrs. Winters answered without turning around as she stood busy at the stovetop. 'Okay Dad, you hurry back.'

I liked it there. There was a good feeling. Everyone was nice and happy. I wondered then if they were always like that or if they were just happy to be leaving and going home.

'Where are you from?' I asked Mrs. Winters.

'We're from Virginia, dear,' she said, turning to offer me a smile and then busying herself with the hot chocolate and soup.

'Are you going back to Virginia?'

'Yes, back home. We're really excited,' she added. 'We've been here four years now. That's enough for me!'

Just as Mrs. Winters turned and brought me a mug of hot chocolate, Nancy came through the doorway and took a seat at the table across from me. Wearing jeans and a loose fitting blouse with flowers on it, she looked at me with a laughing face.

'What're you doing here?' she asked me.

I stared back at her in surprise. Had she forgotten? She couldn't have forgotten. Had she just been joking last night? A girl asking me to give her a kiss was such a rare event that for me, it was not something I could ever forget. Maybe Nancy asked boys to kiss her all the time. Maybe for her this was something completely forgettable, like saying hello or goodbye. Was I going to make a fool of myself here? I picked up the mug of hot chocolate and took a careful sip. I needed more time to think.

'Well, dear,' Mrs. Winters's mother began, 'Tom's come here to help us pack up the car! Haven't you, Tom?'

God bless her.

'Yeah,' I said, thankful for being saved, but also wondering if this would distract Nancy from the subject of why I was really there. She couldn't have just forgotten about last night, could she?

Nancy watched her mother turn around and stir the soup, following her movements with her eyes, thinking about something that was a complete mystery to me. She blinked and turned to me, almost as if she'd just remembered that I was sitting across the table from her. She smiled in a way that seemed to be telling me something, but I hadn't a clue what it might have been. I stared at her, the question on my mind and, I was hoping, in my expression. I was trying to get through to her without actually talking to her. Don't you remember what you said to me last night?

'You're all wet,' Nancy said, focusing on a point in my chest for a moment before shifting her gaze up to meet mine.

'Yeah,' I said, shrugging lightly.

'The poor boy rode his *bike* all the way from Brook-*mule*, dear, in the *rain!*' Mrs. Winters cried, looking at Nancy and shaking her head. She turned to me and smiled apologetically. 'How are you feeling, Tom, are you starting to warm up a bit?'

'Yeah,' I said again. I shrugged again, too. What did I expect? Of course I was the center of attention. I was a cold wet stranger in their apartment.

Nancy had the palms of both hands on her cheeks, staring at me from across the kitchen table. 'Poor thing,' she said softly. Then her hands found a position on the table and she sat up straight. 'Was it fun?' she asked.

Before I could answer, Mrs. Winters sighed and put her hands on her hips and cocked her head to the side. 'Aww, honey?' she complained. 'What do you mean, "was it fun?" Are you trying to make fun of the poor boy?'

But this was just a parents' mistake. Nancy's mother didn't understand that, in fact, it could have been fun to ride five miles in the rain to see someone. Or rather, she had just forgotten about what kids think having fun is. Sometimes.

Mrs. Winters continued to stare at her daughter with a disappointed look on her face.

'No,' Nancy said. 'I wasn't making fun of him.'

Mrs. Winters turned to me, her look of disappointment turning into one of apology.

'Well,' I began, not sure if I should reveal the embarrassing details. 'It probably would have been, but my bike chain broke about half way, so...' I hesitated. Would I tell them about the policeman?

Mrs. Winters' apologetic expression changed to one of dismay. 'Oh, no!' she cried. 'What happened then, did you have to *walk*?'

Americans didn't like walking. They weren't used to it. It was something I never knew that I knew until I left the country and went someplace where they had lots of public transportation that people actually used, every day. They also used their feet.

'Well no wonder you're all wet!' Mrs. Winters cried, her hands now on her cheeks. She turned abruptly and stirred the soup that sat warming in the pot on the stove. 'You need some of this soup now. It's ready,' she said over her shoulder before turning and bringing it over to me, filling a bowl that sat before me with a ladle. I thanked her, picked up the spoon she had placed next to the bowl and started to stir and blow.

'How're you going to get back?' Nancy asked me.

Before I could answer Mrs. Winters gasped and told Nancy that they would give me a ride. 'Would that be okay with you, Tom?' she asked me sweetly as she headed past the table.

'Sure, that would be great,' I told her. She smiled at me and then continued through the living room and disappeared through to doorway leading to the bedrooms, nearly colliding with her daughter Diane.

'Yeah!' Nancy said, just as her big sister Diane, breasts covered now by a tight pink t-shirt, came and sat down right next to her. I caught Nancy rolling her eyes slightly at this intrusion and then turn to look at her sister with raised eyebrows. Diane smiled at me.

'Hi,' she said. My soup spoon was in my mouth at the time. I managed to swallow without choking and returned a feeble greeting to her. I had to use all of my willpower not to see what her breasts looked like covered. I looked her straight in the eye until Nancy sighed loudly and Diane turned to look at her sister. But I guess she was used to catching the roving eyes of boys because as soon as she looked at Nancy she looked again at me and caught me staring at her chest. I looked up at her and then at Nancy.

'What is it, Diane, you want some soup too?' Nancy asked her.

'Yes, maybe I do,' Diane said. She kept her eyes on mine. 'May I?' she asked, reaching across the table towards my bowl.

I sat up straight, left the spoon in the bowl and felt my fingers shrinking back, away from the approaching hands of a woman. 'Sure,' I heard myself say weakly, knowing I was helping Diane to annoy Nancy but not wanting to get in Diane's way either.

'Gross, *Diane*!' Nancy cried, folding her arms across her chest. As Diane drew the bowl across the table and put a full spoon of soup into her mouth, Nancy slammed both palms of her hands flat against the table. 'Mom!' she hollered. 'Nancy's eating Tom's soup!'

Diane thanked me and passed the bowl and spoon back to me. My hands returned to the bowl but I didn't dare eat any of it with Nancy so upset. I looked at Nancy then, expecting to see her eyes boring holes into me, furious that I had allowed her sister to take advantage of her and of me like that, but instead of seeing anger and frustration I saw her eyes wide – with wonder. She smiled at me then and leaned forward.

'Aren't you hungry anymore?' she asked me. 'Go on, eat your soup! You're all wet.'

'Well,' I began.

'Come on, my mom made it for you,' she continued, and then turned to look at her sister, who did not return the gesture but merely sat looking at me with a Cheshire cat grin.

I'm not very brave but when I get annoyed I have a hot temper. I realized the game the Winters sisters were playing and felt heat rising in my face, but somehow I managed to control myself. I took a deep breath. Then another one. I felt more annoyed with Nancy than with Diane, since Nancy should have been on my side. At least, that's how I saw it. I picked up the spoon. 'Yes, I'm still hungry,' I said as I scooped up some soup and took my time eating it and then pulling the spoon slowly from my mouth. I handed the spoon across the table to Diane and drew one arm around the bowl in front of me, protecting it from her. 'Dare you,' I told her, holding the spoon in front of her. Nancy's eyes grew wider and her smile grew broader at this turn of events.

Diane sat up straight and eyed the spoon, her eyebrows raised at my challenge. She looked at me and then again at the spoon, wrinkled her nose, and then stood up. 'Not that hungry,' she said as she turned and once more almost collided with her mother who had returned to the kitchen.

'Oh!' Mrs. Winters cried, 'careful, dear,' she said as she avoided Diane and then began beaming at me again with her big blue eyes. 'What were you complaining about Nance?' she asked Nancy. 'Is the world unkind to you again?'

Nancy sat staring at me, her mouth open. 'What?' she asked her mother absentmindedly. 'Oh. Nothing,' she said. She picked up a paper napkin that sat on the table in front of her and began folding it. 'So, what are you doing here?' she asked me quietly.

The front door opened and two large feet stepped inside the apartment. 'Okay! Car's here! Let's get packed and get on home!'

In the minutes that followed, I helped Mr. Winters to load five suitcases into the back of a shining black Mercedes sedan that he had rented, despite having been offered to have he and his family driven to the airport in one of the army green Chevy Suburbans, just like the one that picked me and my brother up every day in front of our house to take us to the base where we then changed into one of two big army green school busses that drove the whole lot of us to the Munich American High School. 'Are you kiddin'?' he had asked me. 'I want us to get on out of here in style, and besides, for the last four years I've been driving our crappy old Dodge all around Germany. I've been itching to drive some of that German Precision!' Mrs. Winters swooned at how helpful I was as I trudged in and out of the apartment building. Diane had been sitting in the back seat of the Mercedes from the minute her father had announced his arrival. Nancy had gone outside and stood under the shade of a stand of pines that had been planted across the street, creating a miniature forest.

The clouds had mostly cleared and the sun shone down, burning up the moisture all around and causing a misty vapor to rise from the pavement. Carrying the last suitcase down the steps to the door of the building I stopped when I reached the bottom. It had been my intention to change hands, since this was the heaviest of the suitcases I had yet carried. But when I reached the bottom and looked straight ahead, out through the opened door, I saw Mrs. Winters standing in front of me in the middle of the road on the other side of the sleek Mercedes. She was looking to my left. Her expression caused me to pause, and then abandon the suitcase. Stepping past it I stood in the doorway and turned to see what it was that she was looking at. About twenty paces down the sidewalk that ran in front of the BQs, Mr. Winters stood with his back to me. He was talking to someone. With him there, I couldn't see her but I could see from her clothes that it was a woman. Mr. Winters was talking to her in hushed tones but desperation from the both of them was leaking out in tiny yelps. The woman suddenly turned on her heel and strode off. Mr. Winters went after her and grabbed her arm but she twisted free and in that same instant Mr. Winters spun around as well, facing us. His hand went to his face, which had suddenly gone pale and taut. While keeping his head low he shot a glance at his wife and then headed straight for the open trunk at the back end of the car. Looking into the trunk as he drew near the car, he suddenly looked up and around, then at me, and then proceeded directly towards me. His features had begun to soften. I backed up into the building as he approached, my hands raising up in a reflex to hover somewhere just above my waist. Mr. Winters went past me and fetched the suitcase, lifting it as if it were as light as an empty box of tissues.

'Let's get going,' he called out as he placed the final suitcase in the trunk and then slowly lowered the lid to a point where it was electronically retrieved and smoothly and securely shut all by itself as Mr. Winters grinned and shook his head. 'Look at that.' I stepped back outside and stood on the sidewalk next to the car. He looked up at me and smiled, gesturing with his hands to the marvel he had just witnessed. I smiled back at him. He looked over at his wife and nodded. 'Honey?'

Mrs. Winters seemed to stutter then on the first word that escaped her lips. 'Nancy?' she called out, as she turned to look at me instead of her daughter. I caught but then avoided her gaze and instead looked past her at Nancy, still standing in the trees. She was holding some pine needles she had gathered up while standing there, waiting for us to load the car. She took a step forward and let them go, to fall at her feet as she crossed the street and came around to my side of the car. Her mother had already come around and now sat in the front seat of the car next to her husband. Nancy stepped up onto the sidewalk from the road. With everyone else in the car, she kept coming. I thought she was going to crash right into me but she stopped short, rose up on her toes and reached up with both hands to take my cheeks as she kissed me softly on my lips. I closed my eyes but it was already over.

'Are you coming?' she asked me softly.

'Sure,' I told her.